Praise for Ann Warner's Novels

The Babbling Brook Naked Poker Club -Book One

Mystery, nosy old biddies, liars, cheats, romance, intrigue, and lots of human frailty and courage all wrapped into one wonderful read. Janet Tunget

The quirky members of The Babbling Brook Naked Poker Club will charm and inspire you, as they band together to catch a thief. Gail Cleare, author of *The Taste of Air*

A morose parrot with a reputation for biting sits in the lobby of the Brookside Retirement Community, and to Josephine, a reluctant resident, he just about sums the place up. Nick-named Babbling Brook by friend and handwriting expert Lill, the community is to be the setting for art theft, other dodgy dealings and...naked poker. Margaret Johnson, author of *The Goddess Workshop*

Dreams for Stones

Indie Next Generation Book Awards Finalist

...incredibly vivid and emotional tale of love and loyalty, friendship, loss, and faith...*Booklist*

...a lovely story about life changes and love lost and found. *Romantic Times Book Review*

Stunning! Juli Townsend, Author of *Absent Children*

Counterpointe

Endorsed by Compulsion Reads

...a powerful novel of two lovers who face profound challenges. Poignant and insightful...a compelling dramatic evaluation of what it means to love or be loved. *The Midwest Book Review*

...a wonderful exploration of two people from different worlds coming together and finding love and building a lasting, realistic relationship with all the complexities, joys and sorrows that entails. Long and Short of it Reviews

Ann's brilliant, well–thought–out prose lifts her stories to a higher literary level than most of today's fare...prepare to be impressed. Pam Berehulke, Bulletproof Editing

Absence of Grace

...a riveting read of personal struggle, very much recommended. *The Midwest Book Review*

Both a coming of age and a romance novel, this story is captivating and charming. But be prepared, you may not want to put it down once you start. Karen Bryant Doering, author of *Parents' Little Black Book*

...the writing is perfect. Absolutely smooth and divine. Like the best bar of chocolate. Fran Macilvey, author of *Trapped*

Doubtful

Endorsed by Compulsion Reads

Doubtful is a refreshing romance with uncommon depth and enough action and adventure to pull in non–romance readers. I absolutely loved...that both David and Van felt like real people. Compulsion Reads

Doubtful is truly a love story full of intrigue, emotion, and super vivid descriptions of people, places, and things. Delores Warner, author of Don't Buy *Too Many Green Bananas*

Love and Other Acts of Courage

Love and Other Acts of Courage is...beautiful. The plot is engaging and it focused on the development of the characters...and the ending (is) very satisfying. Lorena Sanqui for Readers' Favorite

...a love story woven within an engaging mystery with twists and turns, believable villains, and enough tension to keep you turning pages. Dete Meserve, author of *Good Sam*

...the characterizations of Max, Jake, and Sophie are done so delicately, so perfectly, that each alone would be worthy of a separate story. In short, Love and Other Acts of Courage is so much more than a love story. Kate Moretti, NY Times bestselling author of *Thought I Knew You*

Look for these titles by Ann Warner

THE BABBLING BROOK NAKED POKER CLUB

BOOK TWO

by

ANN WARNER

Silky Stone Press

The Babbling Brook Naked Poker Club - Book Two
Copyright © 2016 Ann Warner
Library of Congress Registration TXu 2-009-950

Edited by
Pam Berehulke, Bulletproof Editing

Cover design by
Kit Foster Design

ISBN 9781723879258

Published in the United States of America

Dedication

To my husband who keeps me feeling young

And to all the wonderful "older" women in my life who have
shown me what it means to age gracefully:
My mother, Evelyn
My grandmothers, Magdalen and Myrtle
And my aunts Josephine and Beth

Here's What Happened in Book One

After her husband's death, Josephine Bartlett is moved into Brookside Retirement Community by her son. Given no choice in the matter, Josephine is well on her way to both feeling and acting miserable when she meets Lill Fitzel who has nick-named the place Babbling Brook in honor of the missing waterway and some of the more irritating residents.

Although Lill is happy to be at Brookside, she sympathizes with Josephine's lack of enthusiasm. Like the unhappy parrot stationed in the lobby, Josephine is liable to bite until Lill begins to smooth her out.

Josephine does accept Lill as a friend but remains careful with relationships, avoiding having people over because hanging in her living room is an Edward Hopper painting. Josephine bought it for several thousand dollars in the seventies, but now the painting could be worth as much as forty million dollars.

Josephine and Lill are invited to join a foursome to play cards. Finding the interactions dull, Josephine suggests they play strip poker, and Lill morphs that suggestion into what they begin to call naked poker: the person with the fewest paper clips at the end of the afternoon has to tell a personal story. Something down and dirty so the others won't forget.

Josephine's story is that when her husband wouldn't allow her to work, she scrimped on the household budget and used that money to buy stocks. She was wildly successful, leading to her husband discovering her activities and forcing her to turn everything over to him. She eventually rebuilt her holdings over the years until she now has sufficient resources she doesn't need any help from her son, who controls her husband's estate.

Through the naked poker group, Josephine and Lill learn that Eddie Colter, Brookside's resident hunk, is stealing from residents by shorting their change when he shops for them. Eddie, or perhaps someone else, is also stealing valuable

1

items from residents: a baseball card, a postage stamp, and a diamond necklace.

Along with Lill, Josephine becomes friends with Devi Subramanian, the associate activities director at Brookside. Devi was previously a curator at the Winterford Art Institute in Chicago but left after an altercation with her then fiancé ended in his death. The death was an accident, but the police asked Devi not to leave the area while they investigated. However, when the fiancé's brother threatens to kill Devi in revenge, she flees and ends up in Cincinnati.

Given her art background, when Devi sees Josephine's painting she recognizes it immediately. That leads to an, at first, reluctant but eventually warm relationship.

When Josephine decides to report the thefts, Devi is the one who accompanies her to the police station, even though Devi is hesitant about being anywhere near a cop.

In this way, the two meet Detective Darren McElroy. Although Mac tells them he can't do much to help with the purported robberies unless someone directly connected reports them, he does agree to speak to Eddie Colter after both women express concerns for their safety. Devi, in particular, has already had to fend off Eddie's unwanted attentions.

Subsequently, Mac becomes friends with Josephine, Devi, and Lill. Divorced two years, he finds himself increasingly attracted to Devi, and his friendship with the three women alleviates his loneliness. Devi is also attracted to Mac, but knows it's best if she keeps her distance.

Once the thefts are officially reported, Mac investigates, but makes little progress. Lill who is a Graphoanalyst suggests to Josephine they might be able to identify the thief by analyzing handwriting samples. She and Josephine collect samples by telling everyone they are putting together inspirational messages for Eddie's daughter who Eddie claims has cancer. In truth Eddie doesn't have a daughter, but that was his excuse when confronted with his grocery shortfalls.

When the book and a ceremonial check for a fund established by another resident are presented to Eddie, he's furious and blames Devi whom he ambushes and attacks.

Devi fights back, and since she has a black belt in tae kwan do, Eddie comes off the worst from their encounter.

That leads him to claim Devi was the aggressor, and he sues her.

Meanwhile Lill has possibly identified the thief, Edna Prisant, one of the naked poker ladies. Before that can be investigated further, Josephine's son visits her unexpectedly. He discovers the Edward Hopper painting and spreads the word about its presence.

After Mac and Josephine move the Hopper painting to safety and Josephine hangs another painting in its place, Lill tries to lure Edna into an attempt to steal the painting. It works. Edna teams up with Eddie to first drug Josephine and then to remove the painting (not the Hopper) and hide it under Josephine's bed. Edna then calls and demands a ransom.

During the ransom payoff, Edna is apprehended and confesses to the theft of the other missing items. Her explanation is that she's done it to help her granddaughter afford a good university. Eddie is implicated as her accomplice but the evidence is circumstantial.

Harry Garrison, the brother, then arrives on the scene. After stalking Devi, he takes a shot at her in front of a bakery where Mac and his neighbor, a five-year-old with Down Syndrome, are having a snack. Mac manages to stop Harry Garrison's second shot, but the first seriously wounds Devi.

While Mac is still at the hospital with Devi, who has barely survived, Lill calls to tell him Josephine is missing. Reluctantly leaving Devi's side, Mac calls his partner for help, and the two discover Josephine has been admitted to a psychiatric facility.

They manage to break her out, but since she's been drugged, she's admitted to the hospital and ends up as Devi's roommate for the night.

During that night, Josephine tells Devi about the man she loved and should have left her husband for, and she pleads with Devi not to let her chance with Mac slip away.

Released from the hospital, Josephine moves quickly to force Eddie to both drop the suit against Devi and resign his position at Brookside.

When Mac takes Devi home from the hospital, she follows Josephine's advice and makes the first move to let Mac know she cares for him.

Chapter One

Devi

Although I'm much improved since I was shot, I still tire easily, and a trip to the Cincinnati airport to drop off my parents exhausted me. They came to stay when I was released from the hospital, but they're both professors at the University of Kansas and they needed to get back for the start of the new semester. Mom said the only reason she felt okay about leaving me was that she knew I had Mac to watch over me.

I took a nap in the afternoon, but I was still feeling draggy when Mac arrived from work, carrying takeout and a bottle of champagne. It was as much New Year's Eve celebrating as either of us thought I could manage.

He set the bag and bottle on the counter, then hugged me carefully. "Did you get any rest today?"

"A little. I doubt I'll make it to midnight, though."

"That's okay. The only new years I seem to usher in anymore are when I have to work a late shift."

"Good to know you aren't rigid in your holiday observances."

Mac's full name is Darren McElroy, and he's a detective on the Montgomery, Ohio, police force. There's a lot we don't yet know about each other, but we're working on it.

We ate the food he brought, and then I moved to the couch and continued to sip my one glass of champagne while he washed dishes. When he finished, he came to sit beside me. His arm curved around me, and I leaned my head on his shoulder.

"I've been wanting to ask you something," he said.

"You've been asking me lots of things lately." I yawned from the effects of the champagne on top of the trip to the airport.

"I know I have. But there's something we haven't talked about yet. And it's maybe premature to bring this up. But..."

"What is it?"

I felt him pull in a deep breath, then release it. "Kids."

My own breath stuttered. I'd been dreading the kids question, although I knew it was coming. Had to come. And it was better to face it sooner rather than later, although it was already too late for me not to have my heart broken if it was a deal-breaker for Mac.

I swallowed. "What about them?"

"How do you feel about them? Do you want any?"

Closing my eyes, I shuddered. "I'm sorry, Mac. I should have told you."

He shifted until he could look at me, but I couldn't face him. I buried my head more deeply in his shoulder.

He rubbed my back. "Told me what?"

"I-I can't have children. The bullet did too much damage, and I..."

His arm tightened around me, and I held my breath waiting for his response, struggling to focus on the steady beating of his heart.

"I'm so sorry, Devi. I expect you wanted them, didn't you."

The tears I was trying to hold back slid down my cheeks. No matter how grateful I was to be alive or how happy I was that Mac and I had found each other, everything hurt when I remembered the surgeon delivering a full accounting of my injuries. He said I'd eventually be as good as new, except for residual twinges that might last for months. And, oh, by the way, I would never have a child.

Every time I let myself think about that, I pictured Mac with his neighbor Teddy. Teddy's five and has Down Syndrome, and Mac clearly loves him. From the first time I saw them together, I could tell Mac would be an exceptional father.

He kissed the top of my head. "It's okay, love. I only asked because—" He stopped, and I waited. "You see, my wife and I—that is, my ex-wife. She wanted kids so badly that when it didn't happen, she..." He heaved in a breath. "And I wasn't sure I could deal with that again. But if you wanted—anyway, you need to know it's okay. Not having any."

I pushed myself upright and stared at him. This was the first time he'd said anything that sounded real about why his marriage failed. When I'd asked, he'd said only that Lisa had a hard time being a cop's wife, and it caused them to grow apart. But this had to be the real reason. And it was huge.

"If you both wanted kids so much, why didn't you adopt?"

"Lisa didn't want to adopt."

"What about you? How do you feel about adoption?"

"Lisa was so set against it; I didn't let myself think about it."

I settled back against his shoulder, shaken at the bleak look I'd seen on his face.

"I'm so sorry." And what an odd reversal it was—this conversation ending with me consoling him, instead of him consoling me.

His arm tightened around me, and we didn't talk at all for a while. Eventually I asked him what his favorite color was. He said purple. And when he asked me in turn, I replied that mine was turquoise.

We continued to talk about mundane things, although every few minutes, we'd stop talking and kiss instead. Somewhere in the middle of either talking or kissing, I fell asleep.

I awakened deep in the night to find Mac's arm still around me and Mac himself sound asleep.

Feeling safe and cherished, I fell back to sleep myself.

Chapter Two

Josephine

Devi and Mac arrived for dinner New Year's Day, both of them with flushed cheeks and sparkling eyes, either from the bitter cold or from inner warmth, and I'd put my money on the latter.

They weren't making any announcements yet, but Lill and I had no doubts they would be soon. Clearly, they were in love, and it did my heart good to see it.

After we were seated and passing food around, Devi turned to me. "Hey, Lillian tells me the man who's filling in for me is single. And attractive."

Devi's the associate activities director here at Brookside Retirement Community. While she's recovering from being shot, a temporary replacement has been hired.

"And he's an art lover. You two should have a lot in common."

I glared at Lill, who looked serenely back. "Now that you and Mac are settled," I told Devi, "Lill's got time on her hands, and she's using it to interfere in my life."

Devi looked startled, but Mac grinned.

"Well," Lill said, "I say Josephine better get on the stick and sign up for an activity or two before Myrtle stakes a claim. You know that Myrtle. She's been in a dreadful tizzy since Norman showed up. Heard the hussy say she thinks he's as dreamy as Harrison Ford."

"Hmmph." In my opinion, the words dreamy and Harrison Ford don't belong in the same sentence. "Myrtle can stake all she wants. I'm not interested. Any more than you'd be if someone *dreamy* like Denzel Washington took over planning our activities."

"Don't know about that. Mm-mmm. If someone who looked like Denzel was doing the planning, I do believe I'd be doing the activying." Lill, who turned sideways would nearly disappear, treated us to that deep, rich chuckle of hers.

"Oh, let Myrtle have her fun."

"Myrtle and Norman...has a nice ring to it, don't you think?" Lill winked at Devi. "I suspect Bertie will be back on the market soon."

That made me snort, and it was a good thing I wasn't sipping wine; I could have aspirated. "What a shame, Bertie being the catch he is." Bertie Teller has been the target of Myrtle's romantic attentions up to now, and I was tired of hearing about it, even if Lill wasn't.

Lill giggled, sounding for a moment seventy years younger than her eighty-two years. And although I'm twelve years younger than she is, I have to work to keep up with her.

"You do realize, Josephine, that if Myrtle turns Norman into her toy boy, we'll never hear the end of it."

"Don't you mean boy toy?" I didn't know Lill even knew the term. Well, obviously she didn't. Exactly. "Oh well. My loss. Besides, I have no interest in meeting another art lover. Hasn't art gotten us all into enough trouble?"

"That wasn't art's fault," Mac said. He and Devi had been watching the volleys between Lill and me with increasing mirth.

"No, of course not," I said. "You know, speaking of art. I've had a thought."

"That's dangerous territory for you, Josephine," Mac said. "Or if not for you, for the rest of us. Leads to all sorts of mayhem. Not to mention extra paperwork for me."

"But you have to admit, *Detective* McElroy, without Lill and me, you never would have caught the Brookside thief." Which was a rather highfalutin way of referring to Edna Prisant.

"I'm willing to concede that. As long as you and Lillian agree to retire from crime fighting."

I sighed. "I don't think we have much choice. Nothing else is happening. It's dreadfully boring."

"Which is precisely why you need something, or *someone*, to spice up your life," Lill said. "And I believe Norman's just the ticket. Besides, he's interested in you."

"What I want to know is why on earth someone named Neumann would saddle their child with a name like Norman?"

"No accounting for white folks," Lill said with an arch look. "Present company excepted."

Lill likes to tease that she and I are Brookside Retirement Community's yin and yang. Or, as she dubs it, the Babbling Brook Retirement Community, in honor of the missing brook and some of the present annoying residents. I retort that instead of the black and the white, we're the black and the gray, and that always makes her laugh.

"You know, Josephine, as improved as Devi's looking, you need to get moving before she comes back to work and Norman leaves."

Devi leaned her chin on her hand and stared at Lill. "What makes you think Norman might be interested in Josephine?"

"Because he's come up to me several times to chat."

"That's certainly a dead giveaway," I said.

"He's noticed we're friends, and since you've been avoiding him, he figures on getting to you through me."

"Really? That's what you think? Well, here's what I think. He's heard the rumors about my painting, and he's looking for a sugar mama."

Lill hooted. "Oh, honey. That's a good one. I'll have to ask Norman about that and see what he says."

"Don't you dare. Really, Lill, this entire conversation is most undignified."

"And to think it started with you having a thought." Mac's lips twitched.

"Yes. That. Well, here it is. But don't say anything right now, Devi. Just think about it, and we'll talk later."

"What is it?"

"I'm thinking about loaning *Sea Watchers* out to museums, and I need someone to coordinate the visits and make all the arrangements." Devi was a curator at the Winterford Art Institute in Chicago before she came to Cincinnati, and she'll know exactly what to do.

She cocked her head and looked like she was thinking, then she straightened and opened her mouth.

"No, don't say anything yet. I know you'll need to think about it. After all, you may prefer to return to your job here at Brookside, and I'm okay with—"

"What if it's yes, I'd love to do that? And, just tell me when I start."

"Hmm, okay. Let's get together this week and work out the details."

Devi and I smiled at each other.

"I like it," Lill said, beaming. "If Devi isn't coming back, it means Norman will have to hang around a while longer."

Chapter Three

Lillian

"We're too old for romance," Josephine told me in a continuation of the conversation started at dinner. Mac had taken Devi home early since she still tired easily.

"You may think we're too old," I retorted, "but spend five minutes with Myrtle and you'll see that's a complete crock."

"What? You mean her rhapsodizing about Bertie? Haven't you had enough of that? I know I have." Josephine snapped the dishtowel and shooed me out of the kitchen, then followed with a tray containing a pot of tea and two cups.

She poured the tea and handed me a cup. "What I want to know is have you talked to Edna lately?"

I considered it a strange segue for Josephine to make. "You know Edna and I are oil and water. Especially after what happened. And don't go trying to change the subject."

"I'm not trying. I am changing it. To Edna. She wants to improve, you know."

"Good for her."

"I think you can help."

"Hmmph. Edna can improve all she likes. I still won't like the woman."

"Graphotherapy?" Josephine stretched out the word and raised her eyebrows.

I'm a certified Graphoanalyst, so I knew what she was referring to. I just wasn't sure why she was bringing it up.

"Edna told me she knows she needs to change, but she doesn't know how to begin. And I thought, if she can be unmasked by Graphoanalysis, perhaps she can be cured by Graphotherapy."

It was an obvious reference to how I used my skill as a Graphoanalyst to figure out that Edna was the one stealing from other Brookside residents.

"Hmm," I said, playing for time. "It does have a certain symmetry, but some people think it's dangerous, you know."

"Dangerous?"

"Well, it does involve tinkering with the psyche. Besides, it isn't a quick or an easy fix."

"I don't think she's looking for quick or easy. And her psyche is precisely what requires tinkering. What I want to know is whether you think it's possible?"

"Of course it's possible. But many things are possible that are improbable. And this is one of them."

"Even if there's only a slim chance it can help, aren't you willing to try? It's the Christian thing to do, after all."

Josephine had me there. I do try to be a good Christian. I sighed. "You can tell her I'm willing to help. But only if she's willing to work very hard."

~ ~ ~

"What did Josephine tell you," I asked Edna when she came at Josephine's behest to discuss Graphotherapy with me.

"Just that you'll help me by pointing out something in my handwriting that needs to be changed. And if I make that change, it will change the way I think."

A good enough explanation for the moment. "And what is it about yourself you want to change?"

Edna frowned and pursed her lips. "I'm not all bad, you know."

Her reaction made me realize I'd sounded like a sour old pickle, but doggone it, the woman was so off-putting.

"I know you don't like me," she said, still frowning. "Mostly people don't, and I don't know why."

"Maybe because you only ever think of yourself?"

"Is that what you think?"

"Yes." Even if she did steal to help her granddaughter go to college, there was still a lot of selfishness in Edna's personality. Something that had been obvious in her handwriting sample.

"I just want to know what I can do to change."

I sighed. "Okay, let me take another look at your writing." I handed her a piece of paper and a pen and told her to write whatever came to mind. "The quick red fox, et cetera. Doesn't matter if it makes any sense as long as you fill the page and write quickly, without thinking about it."

I left her to it, going to my kitchen to make a pot of tea using one of the tea selections Josephine gave me for Christmas. When the tea was ready, I poured Edna a cup, then took my own cup into the living room where I picked up the book I'd been reading.

After several minutes, Edna cleared her throat. "I'm ready."

I walked over to the table, and she handed me the sheet of paper, now covered with writing. As I'd remembered, although I wanted to double-check my impression, her lines of writing slanted down—an indicator of a pessimistic outlook. The letters themselves had a left-leaning slant and a tightness that together suggested she was egocentric, selfish, and probably had a tendency to lie. All were characteristics I'd verified as being true during the time I'd known her.

She also had extended, slightly thicker strokes at the end of many words, something we Graphoanalysts called a club stroke. It's found in the writing of people who have a tendency to push other people away. That also fit the Edna I knew.

No doubt she would find trying to change all those characteristics in one fell swoop impossible and give up. A better plan was to pick one thing and have her work on that a while before she attempted any other changes.

I sat next to her with the paper between us and pointed at the downward slope of her lines. "Here's the first thing I want you to try. Every day, write a page of whatever comes into your head like you did here. But concentrate on making your lines run this way." I used a pencil to draw an upward slanting line on the page. "If you have trouble doing that, add lines that slant up and use them as your template until you can do it without the lines."

"That's all there is to it? It seems so simple."

"Wait until you try it. I think you'll find it's more difficult than you imagine. I'm betting you can write a line or two with an up slant, but as you keep writing, the line will start trending downward as if someone is pulling on your hand. However, if you stick with it, it will get easier. When that happens, pay attention to how you're feeling."

"How long do I have to do this?"

"At least thirty days. But in a week or two, if you're finding it easier, you may be able to add a second modification."

"Oh." She swallowed and chewed on her lip.

"It won't be easy, but it can be worth it, you know."

"And I won't get started any younger, will I." She shrugged. "Anyway, outside of my service assignment, I don't have all that much to do."

"What did they assign you?" After Edna pled guilty to theft, she received a suspended sentence along with community service.

"I'm helping with an after-school program at the elementary school."

"Well, better than digging ditches."

"That wasn't a choice." She caught herself and put a hand up to her mouth. "Oh, you were joking, weren't you."

"I was."

"This is excellent tea." She picked up her cup and took a sip.

"A Christmas present from Josephine."

"I did tell her I was very sorry. For everything I did."

"Yes. She told me."

"And I wasn't a good friend to you either, Lillian. I'm going to try to do better."

"Good. I'm glad to hear it."

She set her cup down. "I guess I should get going and start practicing."

"You may come back when you're ready for more."

I saw her to the door, wondering if her request for help had already begun a change for the better.

For her sake, I hoped so.

Chapter Four

Mac

The phone in the house was ringing when I came in the door, so I grabbed it without checking caller ID.

"Darren?"

It had to be Lisa. She's the only one who calls me that. "Yes? What is it?"

Lisa and I have been divorced two years. Since she's a teacher and I'm a cop, and we didn't have kids or any money left from trying to have kids, there'd been nothing to fight over. It meant our divorce was more a product of exhaustion than acrimony. Since the divorce became final, she's called me only once, and that was to ask about our last tax return.

"I...I need to see you."

"About?" I didn't mean to sound abrupt. But it had been a long time, and she was the one who walked away. So maybe things weren't as free of acrimony as I was telling myself they were.

I rubbed my forehead, then leaned against the wall, waiting for her to tell me what she wanted from me. Hoping to dredge up the generosity of spirit to deal with her gently.

"Please, Darren. I'm here. Can I come in?"

I walked to the front window and looked out. A Honda SUV was parked in front of my house with a woman hunched over the wheel.

I sighed. "Guess I can't convince you I'm still at work."

The woman in the Honda shook her head and looked toward where I was standing.

With a sigh, I told her to come in. When I opened the front door for her, she slid inside with a whoosh of cold air, already pulling off her hat and shaking her hair loose. She reached out, I suspected to hug me, but I stepped back, trying not to appear as uncomfortable and unwelcoming as I felt.

Lisa is a natural blonde with long, tumbling locks I used to curl around my fingers after we made love. At least, in the early days. Before sex became something we scheduled and got through as quickly as we could.

Until I met Devi, whose black hair is as smooth and glossy as a thoroughbred's coat, I would have said blonde was my favorite hair color.

I led the way to my sparsely furnished living room, grabbing a kitchen chair on the way so I didn't have to sit next to Lisa on the couch.

"I saw the article in the paper," she said. "About that man you shot. I was so glad you weren't hurt."

"Yeah, me too."

"So, how have you been, Darren?"

"Fine. I've been fine. What's this about?"

She gulped and looked around the room without apparently seeing it. "I...I'm pregnant."

That staggered me, but for only a moment. "You've remarried?" Although if that was the case, what was she doing sitting on my couch?

She shook her head. "I had an affair. I didn't think I had to worry about birth control, but now..."

"Why are you telling me?"

"I know how disappointed you were, how much you wanted kids. And I thought maybe—"

"No. Don't say it. Don't even think it."

"But you wanted to adopt. Isn't this better?"

"Lisa, we're divorced."

She lifted huge, damp eyes to mine. "That's easily remedied."

My gut twisted. "It's been over two years."

"I know. I'm sorry. I tried so hard to make a life without you. I even..." Her hand curved around a belly that I now noticed was rounded, and her head shook. "Divorcing you was the biggest mistake of my life. I still love you. Are you telling me there's nothing left in your heart?" Tears ran down her face, and her nose was running as well.

Feeling more and more uncomfortable, I got the box of tissues from the kitchen and handed it to her. "I'll always wish you well."

"That's not..." She stopped and shook her head. "I'm going to lose my job, you know."

"Why would you?"

"I teach at a Catholic school now. There's a morals clause. In my contract. An out-of-wedlock pregnancy is a violation."

"I doubt firing you is legal, and for sure it isn't ethical."

She looked away, obviously fighting to control her emotions.

"When are you due?" I knew I was refusing to engage with her on an emotional level, and it saddened me to discover how easy it was to keep my distance.

"May. And I'm so scared. I don't have any savings, you see. And when the job goes, there go my health benefits." She continued to sob intermittently and mop at her face.

I remained sitting on the kitchen chair. A part of me wanted to comfort her, but I knew she'd think it meant I was softening, and it was best for both of us that there be no ambiguity between us.

"So you want..."

"My lease was up. And, well, I found a cheaper place to live, but I can't move in until next week. I was supposed to stay with one of the other teachers in the interim, but she got the flu. So I can't risk staying there. And I really need to save money. For, you know. In case I get fired."

As her words spilled out and filled the room, my gut tightened.

"Lisa, you can't—"

"Please?" She swiped at her eyes and blew her nose. "If I can't stay with you, I'll have to sleep in my car."

I waited a moment to see if she'd say anything more, or if I would. I was tempted to say I'd pay for a hotel for the night but suspected I would end up paying until she moved into the new place.

"Exactly when are you supposed to move into the new place?"

"The, um." She stopped to blow her nose. "The twelfth."

Not next week then, but the week after. Unease made my gut tighten further. The one thing I knew about Lisa after ten years together was that she wasn't always completely open with me. But it was already dark and freezing cold outside, so although I doubted she was telling me the whole story, I couldn't bring myself to turn her away.

"Okay. You can stay here. Until the twelfth."

She raised her head and stared at me with shimmering eyes. "Oh, Darren, thank you, thank you. I knew I could count on you."

I looked at her, my heart twisting in pain at the memory of what we'd once been to each other, but no longer were. If only this pregnancy had happened three years ago, how differently we both would have felt about it. Timing. It's a twisty bugger.

"My things..."

"Are in the car?"

She nodded, and I felt suckered. She'd known I wouldn't be able to turn my back on her; had counted on it.

It wasn't the way I expected to start the new year. And how was Devi going to react to my suddenly complicated personal life? The personal life I'd just begun to share with her.

I moved Lisa's suitcase inside but left the rest of her things in the SUV. I wondered about the furniture she'd insisted on keeping when we split. Had she sold it? Moved it into a friend's garage? I decided not to ask.

After I carried her suitcase into my bedroom, I spent the next thirty minutes changing the bed and shifting my things to the tiny spare room. The house I'm renting is in a section of Blue Ash that's undergoing renewal, and it's on the market. When it sells, it'll be torn down to be replaced by something grander, and I'll have to find another place to live.

Lisa waited in the living room while I got everything arranged. As I finished, she came and stood in the doorway. "Are you working tonight?" she asked.

"No. But I have plans."

"Are you seeing someone?"

"I am."

"Is she nice?"

"Very. I need to get ready. There's food in the fridge and the cupboard. Help yourself."

I walked away from her into the spare room where I collected clean clothes and carried them into the bathroom. I locked the door, and while I showered, I thought about what to tell Devi.

The truth, of course. But would she believe me? Although I was certain what was growing between us was solid, I wasn't looking forward to testing it this soon.

"Mmm, you smell nice," Lisa said as I walked through the kitchen on the way to the garage.

Lisa's sudden appearance had made me forget to call the restaurant to place a takeout order, so I now had to drive there, place the order, and wait. It would mean arriving later than I planned at Devi's, but at least that gave me more time to compose myself before trying to explain to her why my pregnant ex-wife would be living with me for the next nine days.

Chapter Five

Devi

"There's something I need to tell you," Mac said as we finished eating.

Since I've been home from the hospital, Mac has made a habit of bringing over dinner, even though I've told him that while I might not be lifting weights yet, I can lift a cooking pot.

Josephine's theory is that Mac finds it easier to show his feelings through action rather than talk about them. I suspect she's right, and since I assume his bringing me dinner is part of that demonstration, I'm not fighting it at the moment.

"It's about the reason I was late this evening," Mac continued, and I realized my thoughts had drifted as they had a tendency to do of late. "Lisa showed up on my doorstep this evening."

Lisa, as in ex-wife Lisa? That didn't sound good.

"She's...I'm afraid she'll be staying with me for a few days, until she can move into her new place. And," he closed his eyes and his lips firmed, "she's pregnant."

After he said that, he dipped his head into his hands and rubbed his forehead as if it hurt. And I realized I was waiting for more. What I wanted, needed, was to know if he was the father. Because if he was, it would make a mockery of everything I thought I knew about him.

"Is it yours?" I no longer saw any advantage to indirectness. Not since my life so recently hung by a thread. "The baby?"

His head jerked up and then he shook it. "No. No, love. I haven't seen Lisa in over two years. Until today."

"And how long is she staying?"

"Until the twelfth." He glanced at me before once again focusing on his hands, lying on the table between us. "The rest of the story is that she may lose her job. Which means she won't have health insurance when the baby's born."

"But it's got to be illegal to fire a woman because she's pregnant."

"Apparently not if the woman signed a contract with a morals clause."

"Morals clause?"

"She's teaching at a Catholic school."

He stood and walked over to the sink. My thoughts scrambled together as I tried to make sense of what he was saying. That his ex-wife had just moved into his house, and that further, said ex-wife might lose her job and with it her income and her health insurance. So was she really moving to a new place, or was she expecting Mac to support her?

While the Mac I knew and loved wouldn't turn away from helping, I also knew he hadn't yet recovered emotionally from his divorce. Not that I wasn't in equally bad shape. It was the main reason I was taking my relationship with him so slowly.

The other reason I was going slow was economics. Although I'd now accepted the position Josephine offered me on New Year's, I was still waiting for the hospital to tell me what I owed. And I knew I'd need some strong moral support when that happened. Given the hours in surgery and my lengthy stay in the intensive care unit, the bill would be both massive and my responsibility, since I hadn't yet qualified for medical insurance from Brookside.

Mom and Dad had assured me they'd help. And they gave me a large check as a Christmas gift that was currently covering my living expenses. But I viewed the shooting as partly my own fault for letting myself be dazzled by William Garrison. I might not have been blind to William's faults for long, but it was long enough to get engaged to him. When I'd tried to undo that engagement, William brought a gun to the discussion.

In the struggle over that gun, he'd fallen, hitting his head. He'd died a week later, leading his brother, Harry, to search me out and shoot me in revenge. Given that history, it was only right I pay my hospital bill and not shift the burden to my parents. Or to Mac. Perhaps in that way, I'd be able to free myself from my past.

Maybe Mac also had past guilt that taking care of Lisa now would help to lift.

I walked over to him and put my arms around him. "You and I. We sure aren't doing this the easy way."

"What's that?" he said, turning within my arms.

"Falling in love."

"Is that what we're doing?"

"That's what I'm doing." I leaned back and looked at him.

His eyes met mine with that calm *Mac look* that was the first thing I noticed about him when we met. Then he pulled me against him and held me tight.

"Me too," he murmured in my ear.

Chapter Six

Philippa

I opened my laptop, clicked it awake, and after staring at the blank screen for a time, I typed:

???

a novel

by

Philippa Scott Williamson

With that much typed, my stomach clenched.

I lifted my hands from the keyboard and sighed, realizing it was yet another fruitless attempt to write something other than e-mails and brief Facebook posts. They'd been all I'd been able to manage since Richard had his "spell" four months ago, and in its wake, decided we had to move into a retirement community.

"There you are, Philippa. I've been looking for you."

At the fluty tones, I looked up to see a large fluttery woman had wedged herself between the wall and the table where I was working. I closed the laptop, hoping she hadn't read over my shoulder as she approached me.

Frowning, I tried to remember her name. Starts with an...M, a T in there somewhere. Old-fashioned. Ah, yes. Myrtle...Grabby something...

Since moving into Brookside, I've been inundated with names. Names of the five wings, all slightly bizarre flower-bird combinations, and names of residents, most of them too friendly for my taste. The residents that is, not the names.

So, why did I give in so easily when Richard proposed we move here?

Fear, I suppose. It had been terrifying seeing him lying on an emergency room gurney, sweating and grimacing in pain. And even though it turned out to be some sort of blood pressure problem and not a heart attack, it had still left us both traumatized enough that moving to a place like Brookside seemed like a good idea.

For this type of place, Brookside's okay, I suppose. It has wide, carpeted hallways and nicely equipped apartments. The decorative scheme focuses on birds and orchids.

While I'll pass on the birds, there are several large glass-fronted cages of them scattered about, I do like the orchids, which have to be an improvement on the large dusty arrangements of artificial flowers someone told me they've replaced.

Near the front door, there's a smaller cage containing a parrot that looks unhappy to me. The only time I've seen it show any animation was one day when Richard walked by. It perked up and started squawking something that sounded like "pretty boy," making Richard chuckle and throw the bird a salute.

Usually, I stay in the apartment reading when I find writing impossible, but the housekeeper was there this morning. Since I couldn't get either reading or writing done while she swished around vacuuming, dusting, and mopping, I'd moved with my laptop to a corner of the activities center where I sat with my back to the rest of the room to discourage conversation. That obviously hadn't deterred this particular resident.

"Yes. Myrtle, isn't it?" I forced a "say cheese" smile at the woman standing in front of me, wishing I had a wand I could wave to make her disappear.

"Myrtle Grabinowitz."

"Of course. You were looking for me?"

"I was. We need a fourth today. Josephine has begged off. Again." Myrtle sighed theatrically, one hand resting on her considerable bosom.

"A fourth?"

"For cards."

"Sorry. I don't play cards."

"But you're an author, right?"

I nodded, reluctantly. Richard always mentions that fact when we meet people, and while I'm grateful (it no doubt occasionally helps my sales), I also sometimes wish he'd let me be anonymous in social settings.

"This will be perfect then. We play for stories, you see. It was Josephine's idea. Which is why it's so annoying that she rarely plays with us anymore."

I frowned, puzzled.

"We call it naked poker. It's poker, of course. Usually five-card draw or Texas Hold'em. But we use paper clips instead of money, and the person who loses the most that day has to tell a story. A real one. Something down and dirty. And I'm guessing that will be right up your alley."

It sounded appalling. "I'm hazy on how to play any kind of poker."

"We'll teach you. Edna and I had to learn from scratch ourselves. Meet us here at two." And with that, she sailed away, trailing gossamer bits of fabric like an overweight Isadora Duncan.

Short of being rude, I was stuck playing naked poker. I shook my head. The next time the housekeeper came, I'd head to a coffee shop or maybe the nearest branch library.

After Myrtle departed, I carried my laptop back to our apartment, located in the absurdly named Snapdragon Titmouse, or SnapTit, wing, hoping Richard would be there. He wasn't. But neither was the housekeeper, thank goodness.

Richard had left me a note saying he was off to attend one of his LAR, Life After Retirement, classes. It meant if he didn't get back in time, I wouldn't be able to get him to substitute for me in the poker game. Which I was sure he'd be happy to do. Richard's an extrovert and loves interacting with everyone here, something I'm finding exhausting.

Since I was happily alone at the moment, I sat in the recliner, opened my laptop to where I'd left off when Myrtle interrupted me, and tried to decide whether I had any ideas that might be worth pursuing.

I noodled for a time, writing random thoughts, but eventually shut the laptop with a sigh. When was Richard coming home? And what class was he was taking now? Previous choices had been "Samuel Adams – What a Guy," "Music Appreciation from Bach to Bar Mitzvah"—which I found odd since we aren't Jewish—and "Be the Boss of Your Aging Brain."

I glanced at my watch, deciding that since I didn't feel like writing, the most practical use of my time was to spend it in the small gym.

~ ~ ~

When I returned to the apartment from my workout, Richard was back. But when I asked him to take my place in the poker group, he refused, insisting I needed to interact more.

I wanted to stamp my foot in frustration. Instead, shortly before two, I dragged myself back to the activity center where I found Myrtle and two other people waiting for me.

"Over here, Philippa," Myrtle trilled. "Have you met Edna Prisant? And this is Norman Neumann, our new associate activities director."

I nodded at the two and murmured the usual getting-acquainted pleasantries.

Myrtle and Edna are both at least eighty, but Norman looked too young to be trapped in a place like Brookside. Although, as a staff member, he did get to leave every evening.

The "trapped" thought shocked me. I knew I'd been unenthusiastic about the move, but I didn't realize the extent of my resignation and unhappiness until that moment.

"Philippa isn't familiar with five-card draw," Myrtle said. "So I thought we'd start by playing a sample hand so we can show her." Myrtle shuffled while Edna parceled out paper clips.

I glanced at Norman. "Sorry."

"Nonsense. Think nothing of it," Myrtle said. "When Josephine first suggested it, Edna and I didn't know how to play either. But it didn't take us long."

She dealt the cards and talked me through the rules. The trick was remembering what beat what. When I said so, Myrtle lifted a floppy bag onto the table and fished out a piece of paper.

"Here you go," she said, handing me the sheet. "Everything you need to know. Of course, you can still bluff, no matter what's in your hand. So, are we ready to play for real?"

"And whoever loses has to tell a story?" I said, double-checking.

"It's a great icebreaker," Myrtle said. "For example, the first time we played, we discovered Edna tricked her sister's fiancé into marrying her."

"Only because she hurt my dog," Edna said.

I stared at Edna, who looked back steadily. If she was annoyed with Myrtle for blabbing, she hid it well.

"And I'm hoping she'll lose today," Myrtle continued, "because there's a particular story I've been wanting to hear."

Edna cocked her head. "And what story is that?"

"Why, I want to know all about the painting," Myrtle said.

Edna fidgeted, looking less comfortable. I glanced at Norman to see he was focused on Myrtle.

"Painting?" he said.

"Josephine Bartlett has an Edward Hooper painting, and I think Edna knows more about what happened to it than she's telling."

"It's an Edward *Hopper*. And there's nothing to tell." Once again, Edna appeared in control.

I caught my breath in surprise, but covered it with a cough.

"You are familiar with Edward Hopper, aren't you?" Myrtle asked me without missing a beat.

"The name seems familiar."

"Are you certain she has a Hopper?" Norman said. "Here at Brookside?"

Blinking, I transferred my attention to him. He appeared intent. How interesting.

"Well, she did," Edna said. "But it's no longer here."

"See? You do know something," Myrtle said.

"It doesn't take a rocket scientist to figure out once you knew about the painting, she had no choice but to move it," Edna said.

Myrtle glared at Edna, and Edna firmed her lips and looked back.

I noticed Norman, like me, was watching the exchange with an open mouth. I clamped mine shut.

"Do you know which of Hopper's paintings she has?" Norman asked.

Edna shook her head. "I don't have the slightest idea. I never saw it. Now, are we going to play poker or not?"

"Oh yes. Of course we are," Myrtle said, shuffling the cards.

Norman caught my glance and frowned. I decided I'd invite him for drinks sometime soon. Richard would no doubt enjoy meeting him.

When we began playing, I found it more pleasant than I expected. As a writer, I'm a collector of experiences—bits of dialogue, personal stories, and whatever secrets others divulge. It's all fodder, so to speak. And the mention of an Edward Hopper painting was particularly intriguing. A possible story idea?

I might even find a part for Norman. He's quite attractive in that scholarly way that seems to age so well. Myrtle appeared to share my opinion, smiling and fluttering her eyelashes at him, with or without provocation.

His reaction to Myrtle's blandishments was no reaction as far as I could see. I wondered what story he'd tell if he was the biggest loser, something that appeared to be unlikely, given the skill he was demonstrating.

Although hazy on the rules, I knew poker was not just about the cards in one's hand. It was also about "reading" an opponent, and it didn't take me long to classify Myrtle as transparent, Edna as translucent, and Norman as opaque.

Since I didn't care if I lost, I played with abandon and bluffed shamelessly. As a result, Norman and I took turns winning the pots.

Eventually Myrtle collected the cards, and with a sigh, said she guessed she was the one who owed a story. Norman looked across at me and raised one eyebrow a fraction, and I almost spoiled Myrtle's moment by laughing. I'd suspected early on she was losing on purpose, and when she started telling her story, I was sure of it.

It was a rambling account of her experiences in the Miss Ohio pageant back a hundred years ago. But while I found some of the details fascinating—the many uses of chewing gum, for example—the story was mostly a boring ode to a considerably less weighty Myrtle of yesteryear.

"Wasn't this fun?" Myrtle concluded, looking from Norman to me. "We must do it again. Shall we say next Wednesday, same time, same place? Be there or be square."

I decided that although the afternoon had been surprising and not as dull as I'd expected, I had no desire to repeat the experience.

While I searched for words to ease myself out of any further obligation to play naked poker, Norman spoke. "I'm sorry. I have to be so careful about invitations. Don't want to be accused of playing favorites."

"And I'll be writing," I said, tacking onto Norman's statement with a sigh of relief. "On a deadline, you know." His words had been much more straightforward than the mealy ones I'd been organizing. It's an ongoing frustration that I can write characters who are assertive and tough, but I fall short in real life.

Myrtle sat for a moment, her mouth hanging open, and I was tempted to lean over and push it shut.

"But I do want to thank you for a most interesting afternoon." Norman stood, then with a quick nod to each of us, he turned and walked away.

"My goodness," Myrtle said. "Aren't we lucky he played with us at all."

It was my turn to blink in surprise at Myrtle's neat swivel to put a positive spin on Norman's obvious rejection.

I decided the best ongoing strategy was to continue to follow his lead. Standing, I thanked them and walked away. Like Norman—without looking back.

Chapter Seven

Josephine

At Lill's knock, I grabbed a sweater and together we walked to the dining room. Sometimes we sit with a group at dinner, but this evening, we chose a table set for two.

After we seated ourselves, Devi's replacement walked up to us. Lill greeted him enthusiastically.

"I wonder if I might join the two of you?"

I frowned at him. "There are only two places."

Lill kicked me under the table, and let me just say right up front that it's one of my least favorite forms of communication from her, even though it is effective.

"Please do," Lill said.

Our waitress hurried over with another place setting, and the man snagged a chair from an empty table. He held out a hand.

"Norman Neumann."

I'd been bingeing on *Downton Abbey* and decided to channel Maggie Smith at her most imperious. "Mrs. Bartlett. And you want to join us because?"

"Making the rounds. I'd like to get to know all of you."

"Who have you met so far?" Lill asked, obviously trying to counter the chill.

31

I examined Norman Neumann, withholding any approval of his presumptuous presence. I didn't think he was dreamy, nor did I think he looked the least like Harrison Ford, but age did become him the way it does so many men and so few women.

"I played naked poker with three people just this afternoon," he said.

"Did you?" I said.

"I did. Understand you invented the game."

"I don't think so. Poker's no doubt been around a millennia or two. Who lost?"

"Myrtle Grab..." He shook his head.

"Grabinowitz. And I'm guessing she treated you to her 'almost Miss Ohio' story?"

"She did."

Lill chortled, and Norman smiled at her. "Edna Prisant was there too, and Myrtle goaded her. Something about a painting—"

"How interesting." I smiled at the waitress who'd just delivered our salads, and I moved my leg so Lill couldn't whack me again.

"An Edward Hopper. Although she called it an Edward Hooper."

"She would," I said. "Who else was playing?"

"Philippa Williamson."

"The author."

"Is she?"

"Quite famous, I believe. What career path did you follow, Mr. Neumann? I understand this is only a temporary position for you."

"Please, call me Norman. I'm...I was a forensic accountant. And yes, I'm just filling in."

"So in your former life, did you root out corruption on Wall Street?"

"Something like that."

"Why leave that to do this?"

He blinked at me, and the pause gathered momentum.

Lill cleared her throat but I avoided looking at her. Instead, I took a bite of salad and watched Norman do the same. Then he looked up as if surprised the question still hovered.

"Forensic accountant to retirement community associate activities director?" I prompted. "Rather an odd second act."

"My...wife was ill. It forced me to rethink my life."

I glanced at his hands. No ring was in evidence and he was reputed to be single, so perhaps she'd died? "I'm sorry for your loss."

"As am I," Lill added, giving me a stern look. I could tell the words she was biting on were, *For Pete's sake, Josephine. Give the poor man a break.*

"Did you make any major busts? That is, during your accounting career?"

"I did."

"Enron? Bernie Madoff?"

"Nothing that big." He looked up with a grin. "But if I'd had you on my team asking the questions, who knows."

"Yes. Josephine is quite adept," Lill murmured.

"Do you know about the Hopper painting?" he said, turning his attention to Lill.

"Oh my, yes. Josephine and I are great friends."

I finished my salad and sat back to watch the two, amused that he was questioning Lill about me, in front of me.

"Is it still here?"

"Afraid not. Once word got out, Josephine knew she had to hide it."

"Do you know where it is?"

The waitress interrupted us, coming to remove our salad plates so she could deliver our entrees.

Lill waited until the waitress had moved on to another table. "I don't know where the painting is. But Josephine does. As does Mac."

I kicked Lill. A first for me. She was being entirely too free with information. My information.

"Who's Mac?"

"A friend of ours." Lill responded. "He's a detective in the local police department." She moved her foot, then looked up and grinned at me before continuing to address Norman. "That's old news, of course. Along with Josephine and me being the ones who figured out who was stealing valuables from residents. Not to mention the shooting of your predecessor."

Norman stared at her. From his dazed expression, I knew he was trying to figure out if she was pulling his leg.

"Indeed," I said. "Brookside isn't as dull as it may at first appear."

Norman looked at me, then at Lill, and chuckled. "How about those Bengals, huh?"

"If you're looking for a Bengals fan, you won't find one at this table," I said.

Once again he shook his head. "What career paths did the two of you follow?"

"I was a math teacher in the Cincinnati public schools," Lill said.

"And a Graphoanalyst," I reminded her.

"But that wasn't until after I retired. The first time."

"Lill worked with the police and a large international company based in Cincinnati. But if she tells you which one, you might be accused of insider trading."

Lill shook her head at me. "Josephine."

"How about you, Mrs. Bartlett?" Norman said.

I found it strange he hadn't graduated to our first names, although I hadn't invited him to. But his formality about that was in direct contrast to his intrusive questions.

"Freelance investor."

"Don't forget art connoisseur," Lill added.

"Are there others here like you two?"

"Nope. We're both originals," Lill said.

"I suspected as much," he said.

~ ~ ~

After offering Devi the position as my art consultant, I called the Cincinnati Art Museum in early January and made an appointment with the director, Miriam O'Pinsky. I'd met her briefly as I'd still been on the board when we lured her away from Tulsa.

"Josephine. How nice to see you again," Miriam said, welcoming me to her office. "I was so sorry when you had to resign from the board. Your husband was ill, I believe?"

"Yes. He died last August."

"I'm so sorry to hear that."

"Yes, umm." Since I don't miss Thomas, I always struggle with what to say when someone offers me condolences.

"Would you like tea?" Miriam was obviously skilled at bridging awkward conversational gaps.

I said that would be lovely, and while we waited for it to appear, she told me about the museum's most recent special exhibit and what she was planning for the future.

"One reason I asked to meet with you," I said after taking the first sip of an excellent cup of oolong tea, "is that I was wondering about your staffing levels. Do you have a sufficient number of curators?"

"We never have as many as we would like, of course. But with current funding, we're not doing too badly."

"What about planning for new programs?"

"I have to admit that's an area where we're weak at the moment, and we don't have the funds to do much about it."

"Let me see if I have the translation correct. You're not only short on curators, but your planning group is struggling with inadequate staffing."

"Close," she said with a smile. "It's our usual condition, I'm afraid. We do the best we can, of course. The grant that covers free admission has been a godsend as it allows us to plan our budgets more effectively. But then in some ways it's also tied our hands. But surely, you're not here to talk about my staffing issues."

Actually, I was. But I knew I had to move carefully. It was possible Miriam would be resistant to what I was planning.

"I wanted to verify my impressions, of course, but I don't want you to think I'm here in an unofficial capacity to second-guess you."

"I didn't think that." She smiled. "Ed let slip you were the member on the board who was most supportive of me, even though I was pregnant when I came to interview. And I'm most grateful."

"And your child?"

"She's nearly two. My husband and I love Cincinnati. We hope to stay here permanently."

"I'm glad to hear it."

"So, why are you here?" she said.

Her directness had been one reason I'd supported her. In her interview, she'd done a good job of articulating what she saw as the difficulties of the position while other candidates had sought to win us over with flattery.

"I'm here to ask if the museum would be interested in a second Edward Hopper."

She blinked. "Wow. Of course we would. But you know our budget for acquisitions is always tight. Which painting?"

"*Sea Watchers*. And I don't want to sell it. It's part of a trust that will eventually pass to the museum. But in the meantime I'm looking for a home base."

"With conditions, of course?" She sat back and took a sip of tea.

"Of course." This was a huge step for me, and it relieved me to see Miriam realized that and was granting me space to present my case. "I want the painting to spend most of the time in Cincinnati. But I also want to loan it to other museums."

"Would you arrange that, or would you expect us to?"

"I know it can be a difficult and time-consuming effort. And a drain on your already stretched resources."

"True. On the other hand, it would be a major coup for this museum to be the permanent home for *Sea Watchers* sooner rather than later."

"Here's what I'm thinking. I can hire someone to be in charge of the painting, arranging for its visits elsewhere, but since that won't be a full-time job, and you need additional help on your staff..."

"Ah. I see. A joint appointment. How much of a commitment do you want from us?"

"Office space, an appropriate title, and duties."

"Salary and benefits?"

"I'll provide that through a grant."

"You have someone in mind for the position?"

"I do." I pulled the printout from my purse and handed it to her. "Forgive the formatting. She didn't put that together; I did."

Miriam took the pages and leaned back, reading. Then she looked up with a frown. "I believe I've been in contact with Ms. Subramanian. Last year. She was organizing an exhibit of twentieth-century painters for the Winterford in Chicago. We agreed to lend our Grant Wood to the exhibit. The arrangements were complete and we were getting ready to ship the painting when I suddenly found myself dealing with a different person who refused to explain why Ms. Subramanian was unavailable."

Nervous about where I could see her going, I concentrated on sounding calm. "I can tell you the reason for that. What happened is that Devi was involved with a man who didn't want to break up with her. He threatened her with a gun, and in the ensuing struggle, he fell, hit his head, and later died."

Miriam sat blinking at me.

"The man's brother blamed Devi and threatened to kill her. She left Chicago in fear for her life. Justified, it turns out, since a couple of months ago, the brother tracked her here and shot her. She's still recovering."

"My goodness." The words had a breathy quality, and I could tell from her expression she was trying to figure out a way to extricate herself from accepting Devi as part of her staff.

I spoke quickly to head her off. "I know all of that has to be concerning, but you have my assurance Devi has my full confidence."

Miriam read through the pages I'd given her again before raising her head and giving me a direct look. "Before I take any further steps on this offer, I want to meet her."

"Of course. Best to do that at my place, don't you think?"

"Yes, I believe so."

"I'll arrange something and let you know then."

She nodded. "Good. That will also give me time to think about your proposal."

Although she'd obviously been excited about the possibility of adding a second Hopper to the museum's collection, it was equally clear she was unenthusiastic about the rest of my plan.

All I could hope was once she met Devi, she would change her mind.

Chapter Eight

Devi

Arriving at Josephine's to discuss the final arrangements for my new position brought back a wash of memories, including our adversarial initial meeting that had also included my first glimpse of *Sea Watchers*.

When Josephine opened the door, my gaze went immediately to the spot where the painting used to hang. In its place was the Domenic Demeri watercolor. Although I thought the landscape was lovely, and Demeri was obviously a skilled artist, I did miss the Hopper, which was the more challenging and intriguing image.

"You look better every time I see you," Josephine said, smiling at me. "I thought we'd celebrate your recovery with the Lapsang souchong tea you like."

"Wonderful."

The tea, already brewed, was in a pot on the coffee table along with a short stack of papers.

She poured us both cups, then sat back and examined me. "You're definitely looking less fragile. I'm so happy to see it. As is Mac, I'm sure."

"I believe so." I smiled at her obvious attempt to grill me. Josephine can be direct but she can also be subtle, and after giving both Mac and me hefty shoves in each other's direction, she'd recently backed off into subtle territory.

"Any news on Harry Garrison?" she asked. Harry Garrison is the man who shot me.

"Mac said the prosecutor is drawing up a plea deal. Given a police officer witnessed the shooting, nobody expects Harry to turn it down."

"How many years?"

I shook my head. "That's still being resolved. But the charge will be attempted manslaughter."

"Even though it was obviously attempted pre-meditated murder?" Josephine's words were clipped and stuffed with outrage while I felt more sad than angry. Perhaps when I had more energy, I'd be angry.

Josephine shook her head with a sharp movement. "Do let's talk about something happier." She set her cup down and picked up the papers sitting on the table. "We need to iron out your employment details." Pulling off the top few pages, she handed them to me. "This is your employment contract. Take your time to go over it." She then told me what she proposed as a starting salary including medical benefits, more than I'd been making at the Winterford.

The position provided the perfect way for me to resume following my dreams in the art world, after being sidetracked most of the last year by Harry's threat.

There was a knock on the door. Josephine didn't look surprised, and when she ushered the visitor in, I understood why.

"Devi, I believe you know Miriam O'Pinsky, although she tells me you've never met in person."

"Yes. So nice to meet you at last, Miriam."

Josephine hung Miriam's coat in the closet, then gestured toward a seat and poured a cup of tea for the visitor.

"Devi and I were just discussing the terms of her employment," Josephine said as the three of us settled ourselves.

Miriam turned her attention to me, giving me a thorough once-over. "Josephine tells me you were recently shot, and it was related to your departure from the Winterford?"

"Yes. And I owe you an apology for leaving you hanging without an explanation."

"She said you were in fear of your life?"

"I was."

"Your fear appears to be justified."

I nodded, wondering why she was questioning me this way.

"Did you like working at the Winterford?"

"I loved it. I miss it."

"The director and I spoke this morning. He told me he invited you to return."

Again, I nodded. This was sounding more and more like a job interview. But I already had a job, or I would have as soon as I signed the contract with Josephine.

"But you turned him down?"

"I've made a new life here."

"So you intend to stay in Cincinnati?"

"Yes. I've just accepted a position here."

"Is it one you expect will fulfill you on a professional level?"

"I...only partly, I'm afraid." I glanced at Josephine, who was sipping tea with a calm expression. I was coming to a conclusion about this meeting; I just hoped it was the right one. "You see, while it's a challenging position and I'm going to enjoy it immensely, there will be stretches of time when I'll have very little to do."

"Do you have a plan for that available time?"

"Not yet."

Miriam nodded at Josephine. "You had me at *Sea Watchers*, of course. But the real clincher was the Winterford wanting Devi back. That's the highest recommendation in my book. I did still want to meet you, however." She looked back at me.

"Good." Josephine sounded brisk. She tipped her head from Miriam toward me.

"Devi, I'm very much hoping you'll spend your extra time with us at the Cincinnati Art Museum. And in that regard, it's my pleasure to offer you the position of Curator of Special Projects."

I looked from Josephine to Miriam and then at the contract I hadn't yet read. The joint offer was a dream position. Even better than the one at the Winterford I'd had to give up.

"If it's all right with Josephine?" I looked at her and she nodded. "Then I'm delighted to accept your offer."

Chapter Nine

Philippa

I was in the gym doing my daily workout when a woman I hadn't yet met arrived and climbed on the exercycle next to the elliptical trainer I was using. I pulled out my earbuds and slowed my pace, and we greeted each other and exchanged names. Hers was Josephine.

"Ah. I heard your name taken in vain the other day."

She was busy setting up a program on the cycle, but she glanced at me with a questioning look.

"Myrtle Grabinowitz. She coerced me into playing naked poker. She said you invented the game."

"Hardly. You mustn't let Myrtle make you do things you don't want to do, you know. It can be exhausting, otherwise."

"It was okay, but I wouldn't want to make a habit of it."

"I heard about the game."

"You did? From whom?"

Josephine frowned. "Norman Neumann. He joined Lill and me at dinner the other evening. He said Myrtle treated you to her 'almost Miss Ohio' saga?" Pedaling, she clicked the final button.

"I liked the part about the chewing gum."

"It is the best part, isn't it? And what makes it even more amusing is that it was Miss Congeniality's idea."

"Do you think she knew what could happen?"

"I suspect so. But I have only Myrtle's account. Who knows at this late date? I heard you're a writer?"

"Yes."

"Do you enjoy writing?"

"Yes, I do."

"So you don't buy into suffering for your art?"

"Certainly not."

We smiled at each other, then I slipped my earbuds back in and kicked up my intensity. Josephine did the same.

Chapter Ten

Mac

Since Lisa showed up, I'd been avoiding my house, going directly from work to spend the evenings with Devi, then coming home late for short, fitful nights of sleep. Lisa leaves early in the morning, which makes it easy to avoid her, but her moving around to get ready means I don't sleep much past five, and after a few days of this schedule I was tired. But the thought she would be moving soon kept me bucked up.

Or maybe she wasn't. In the past three days she'd steadily transferred stuff from her car to the house, and when I said something about it making the move to the new place more arduous, she simply shrugged.

Friday night, which was supposed to be her last before the move, I arrived home from Devi's after midnight to find Lisa waiting up for me.

"Darren, we need to talk."

"Do you need my help moving tomorrow?"

"About that. The new apartment fell through. And I had to tell the school something, so I gave them this address. And when I was talking to the principal about that, she noticed I was pregnant. And she made the assumption we'd...well, they do know me as Mrs. McElroy, after all. And I sort of let her think—"

"That you and I are still married?"

"Remarried. I'd told them we divorced, so it had to be a remarriage."

"And when and how did we manage that?" The words pushed out from behind gritted teeth.

"Five months ago. In Mexico. We eloped, right before school started. But I thought to be safe, we need to—"

"No." I closed my lips over other words. Angry words. Frustrated words.

"But, Darren—"

"I'm providing temporary shelter. That's it. You need to find another place to live and a way around this that doesn't involve me."

"But I told her—"

"Maybe you need to go to confession."

I walked away because in that moment, it was essential to my peace of mind to do so. But my house isn't big enough to avoid a problem as large as a pregnant ex-wife.

~ ~ ~

After another few days of struggling to sleep on sofa cushions, I accepted that the arrangement with Lisa wasn't going to end as soon as I'd hoped, and I bought a mattress. By the time it was delivered, my lack of sleep had accumulated to the point I was irritable with coworkers, something Dillingham noticed since we're partners. He didn't let it fester, one of his better qualities.

"What's going on, McElroy? You and Devi aren't having problems, are you?"

Dillingham was driving, which was good, because my concentration was shot. We were on our way to back up a patrol unit dealing with a domestic disturbance.

"That may be the one part of my life that's still working."

"What then?"

"Lisa."

"Uh-oh." Dillingham and I have worked together long enough he both knows Lisa and doesn't particularly like her. "What's up with the princess?"

"She's pregnant."

He shot me a quick glance before focusing back on his driving. "Not yours, I take it?"

"No."

"Then why is it your problem?"

I explained about the morals clause and Lisa's need to stay with me while she searched for a cheap place to live, although I was beginning to doubt she was even looking.

"Doesn't get much cheaper than free," Dillingham said. Which, unfortunately, was too true. "So, you're what? Back together?"

"We're not together, together. She's just staying at my house until she finds a place."

"And you're staying...?"

"Also at my house."

He whistled. "That's got to be awkward."

"And exhausting. I don't think I've had a good night's sleep since she moved in."

"Why don't you move in with Devi? That's where you're heading, am I right?"

"I hope so."

"So?"

"Devi's old-fashioned, or her father is. I don't want to make her uncomfortable."

"Then marry the girl."

"It's not that simple."

"Why not? Seems simple to me."

"She needs time to recover from...everything. And to think about things."

"Did she say that?"

"Not exactly."

"So what you're saying here is you need time to recover and to think about things."

"Lisa wants us to remarry."

"What?"

"That way she can keep her job and her medical insurance. We'd divorce as soon as the baby is born."

"I get it. Like a green-card wedding. You're not seriously considering it?"

"No. Of course not."

That didn't come out as strongly as it should have, and Dillingham jumped on it.

"I certainly hope you're not. If that isn't the very definition of a harebrained scheme, I don't know what is." Once again, he glanced at me. "You know what I think? If you were sleeping good, you'd come up with a better solution. At the least, marrying Lisa so she can keep her health insurance has to be unethical. At the most, it's probably illegal. So that's my prescription. Sleep on it. And more than eight hours. If necessary, spend a couple of nights in a hotel. Or better yet, come home with me. We've got a spare room."

As generous as the offer was, and as much as I liked Dillingham's wife, they're newlyweds, and knowing they were in the next room would be even less conducive to a good night's sleep than my new mattress.

Before I could tell Dillingham that, we arrived at our destination to find the situation had escalated. The husband had a gun, and he'd barricaded himself inside the house with one of his kids.

That was good in a way because while dealing with it, I didn't have time to worry about my own problems.

Chapter Eleven

Devi

This was my second call to the hospital's billing office. When I'd called before, I'd been bounced around without getting a clear answer about the status of my bill. Today, I finally reached someone who told me it would be mailed at the end of the month.

Not that I was looking forward to receiving it, but the sooner it arrived, the sooner I could set up a payment plan. I pushed, and the woman I was talking to took my address and promised to print out a copy and send it.

It arrived the next day. Taking a deep breath, I skipped to the last page. The final six-figure total was breathtaking. But then I realized a payment offset that number, and the amount owed was zero.

I stared at that line—amount owed—thinking about the implications. Josephine must have paid it, and even though I knew she could afford it, it made me uncomfortable given everything else she'd done for me.

I debated how to thank her, and only one possibility came to mind.

Josephine is a tea aficionado. So much so that I doubt anything I could afford would fit her exacting standards, but she also enjoys cookies with her tea—the ones from Servatii's bakery. Servatii's is where I was shot, and the thought of going there instantly dried out my mouth and made my stomach cramp. But with this latest proof of Josephine's generosity staring me in the face, daring me to act, I ignored my discomfort, put on my coat, and went out and got in my car.

It was snowing, but snow wasn't the reason I drove slower and slower until finally the driver behind me lost patience and honked. I pulled over to the curb and sat waiting for the shakes to subside, knowing that if nothing else, I needed to prove to myself I could do this. There was nothing to fear, after all. Harry Garrison was in jail and would be for years.

After repeating that several times, I managed to get moving again.

The last time I came here, I'd parked right in front of the bakery, against the curb, and Harry Garrison had pulled in behind, trapping me. This time I parked in the middle of the lot with the car positioned so it was ready to drive off.

After more deep breathing, I climbed out of the car. My doctor had told me to avoid icy conditions until I healed completely as he didn't want me falling. That meant I needed to concentrate as I made my way around the patches of snow and ice. The good thing was that kept me distracted all the way to the bakery's door.

Arriving there, I glanced at the spot where I'd fallen, wondering if there was a bloodstain underneath the snow. Shivering, I opened the door and stepped into warmth filled with the good smell of fresh baking and cinnamon.

The woman behind the counter smiled and asked if she could help me—exactly as she'd always done. That fragment of normality eased my way, and I was able to behave like being there was nothing out of the ordinary. I chose a loaf of bread to share with Mac at dinner and a selection of Josephine's favorite cookies.

Back in the car, I sat for a time breathing heavily as if I'd just finished a vigorous run. When I was finally calm, I drove to Brookside and used my employee code to open the back door. Once inside, I knocked on Josephine's door.

I'd been obsessing so much over the visit to the bakery, it didn't occur to me until that moment that Josephine might not be home. But the snowy weather must have been keeping her in because she answered the door promptly, grinning when she saw me.

"What a lovely surprise. And just in time for tea."

I suspect for Josephine any time is just in time for tea.

"I've brought cookies." I handed her the box.

"Wonderful. I've been missing these. But to tell you the truth, I couldn't bring myself to go there after what happened. I suspect it wasn't easy for you either?" She turned to set the cookies on the table.

"No. But I'm glad I did it."

She turned back and gave me a solemn look. "I'm glad you're glad." Then she did a very un-Josephine-like thing. She hugged me before bustling away to start the kettle heating while I removed scarf, gloves, hat, and coat.

After we sat down with our tea and cookies, I pulled the hospital bill out of my tote. "Once again I owe you." I handed the bill to Josephine.

She glanced through the pages, then looked at me and shook her head. "You think I paid this?"

"Who else do I know who could afford it?"

"You must know somebody, because this wasn't me. Although I would have been happy to do it. Hmm. You know, I don't believe you were supposed to receive this." She tapped a finger on the first page, pointing out where a Ronald and Emily Garrison were listed with a Chicago address. "Harry and William's parents?"

"But why would they do that? Because of me, one of their sons is dead and the other's in prison."

"Oh, Devi. They lost their sons because those sons made dreadful choices. They have to realize that. They may be trying to make it up to you for what those sons put you through."

"Do you think I should thank them?"

"No. I think you should let it go. If they'd wanted you to know, they would have told you."

Her words left me feeling troubled, but also relieved.

That bill had been one thing coming between Mac and me. And its shadowy menace had been growing ever larger since Lisa's re-entry into his life.

Now, with that worry lifted, maybe Mac and I could figure out what to do about the other difficulties we faced.

~ ~ ~

When Mac arrived this evening, I poured him a beer and handed it to him along with the bill. With a sigh, he sat at the table and read through the pages. Then with a puzzled look, he waved them at me.

"Does this mean what I think it does?"

"What do you think it means?"

"You owe nothing? How did that happen?"

I walked over and picked up the first page and pointed at the Garrisons' names. "I thought Josephine paid it. But she didn't. She's the one who noticed this."

"I see. It's fair, though. That they paid. Are you okay with it?"

"I'm still pinching myself to make sure I'm awake. It makes me uncomfortable, but yes, I'm mostly okay with it."

He squared up the pages and folded them back in the envelope, then he looked up and grabbed my hand as I walked by to get the casserole I'd fixed for our dinner out of the oven.

"Devi, there's something I need to talk to you about. I've been putting it off, and I apologize for that."

Whenever something worries or alarms me, the spot where the bullet went in feels like it's been poked. I try not to gasp, though, because it worries Mac whenever I have a pain. "What's going on?"

He led me over to the couch and we sat next to each other, our knees touching.

"It's about Lisa."

He rarely mentions Lisa, so neither do I. I know from how much time he spends with me that he's avoiding her as much as he can, and that reassures me. But it doesn't mean the stitch in my side doesn't still hurt whenever I think about her in Mac's house.

"She told the people at her school we'd remarried. As for the new apartment, it supposedly fell through, but I suspect she lied about that as well."

If I hadn't already been sitting, I would be now. Without realizing I was doing it, I pressed against my side, trying to ease the bolt of pain.

"Are you okay?"

I shook my head. "Just a couple of nerve endings kicking up. And you're kidding, aren't you? About Lisa?"

He shook his head. "I wish I were. But nothing about this situation is remotely kid-worthy." He closed his eyes, opened them, and took a breath. "Sorry. That didn't come out quite right."

"I don't know. I thought it was pretty good."

He looked up, and I smiled at him. After a moment, he tentatively smiled back. "You're right. We've both been—"

"Letting our respective situations get to us? Forgetting to laugh? Forgetting we're basically okay and we have each other?"

"Yes. All the above. So, what do we do about my situation?"

"I can think of a couple of things." Maybe he should be saying this. But this was, after all, the twenty-first century. "Why don't you move in with me? You're already here most of the time anyway, and—"

He reached out a finger and placed it on my lips, stilling the words tumbling out faster and faster. He cocked his head, examining me and, for the first time in a while, he exuded that sense of calm competence I noticed the first time I met him and that I find so appealing. I reached out and squeezed his hand, remembering what it had been like before I could touch him freely like this.

"Devi, love, that's one of the nicest offers I've ever had."

My heart began to pound. "But...? There is a but, isn't there."

"I don't want to start our life together with a spur-of-the-moment decision made for the wrong reason."

Start our life together? I cleared my throat. "The wrong reason?"

"I don't want what we do to be driven by what's happening with Lisa."

"It is, though. Whether we like it or not. She's the elephant in every room, Mac, even though we barely mention her. But telling people she's married to you...isn't it obvious she's trying to maneuver you into taking care of her permanently?"

"Don't you think I know that? I want her out of my life. But I don't know how to go about it in a reasonable, compassionate way."

"Doesn't she have a family?"

"A sister is all. Kendra is a photojournalist, so she travels a lot."

"Does Kendra have a home base? An apartment maybe?"

He shook his head. "She lives with her partner. In New York. They're lesbians. Lisa wasn't very nice to Kendra when she first found out. Since then, they don't have much to do with each other."

"What about friends? Doesn't she have any?"

Again he shook his head, rubbing his forehead. "Funny, I didn't realize until this came up that Lisa has so few friends and none that live in this area."

"So, it's back to my offer."

"I seem to remember a story about a girl with a traditional father who is rather traditional herself. Or was that just an excuse?"

He was referring to what I'd told him about my brief engagement to William Garrison. After asking me to marry him, William had pressured me to move in with him. I'd refused, telling him I couldn't until after the wedding because I didn't want to upset my father.

"It's true. So you know it's not every day I invite a strange guy to live with me."

"Strange? What's strange about me? Didn't Lillian say we're a perfect match? So if I'm strange, you must be too."

"Not necessarily. It could be that although perfectly normal, I'm attracted to your strangeness. At any rate, being strange isn't a deal-breaker for me, you know." I couldn't remember the last time I'd gotten Mac to spar with me in such a lighthearted way. For sure, not since Lisa arrived on the scene.

"You do realize if you move in now, there's no performance pressure. I can't have sex for at least another month. Meanwhile, we could work on other compatibilities...movies, music, books, popcorn—with or without butter—amount and type of sports watching, level of acceptable environmental chaos, choice of pets—"

"Money, religion, politics?"

I checked to make sure he was teasing, and knew he was from the glint in his eyes.

"Only if you insist."

"I do." His lips settled into an almost smile.

"Okay. I'm a penny-pincher, a Buddhist-leaning Christian, politically an Independent. I make my bed every day, hang up my clothes as I take them off, and I like to read in bed, but I never eat in bed. And I prefer dogs to cats or gerbils. Or birds." I gestured toward him, hands open. "Your turn."

He reached out and ran a finger over one of my wrists, making me smile.

"Hmm. I'm careful with money, but I don't consider myself tight. Raised Lutheran, but I rarely go to church because, in my opinion, religion causes more problems than it solves. I'm generally fed up with politicians of both parties, but I keep that opinion to myself because I work with a couple of rabid Republicans. I make my bed most mornings and usually put my clothes in the hamper when I take them off. I can give up eating in bed. Most definitely dogs."

I scooted closer and leaned against him, and his arm settled around me. He blew a soft breath into my hair, and I let go of all my Lisa angst. At least for the moment.

As for Mac, although willing to engage in verbal play, he was still adamant about going back to his own place at the end of the evening.

That reignited the angst. Sighing, I tamped down on it, knowing I didn't need to add any more drama to either Mac's life or my own.

Chapter Twelve

Philippa

To placate Richard about my lack of interactions with other residents, I invited Josephine and her friend Lillian for drinks. I included Norman for Richard's sake, then I thought about it some more and added Myrtle and Edna.

While I told myself their addition was to ensure the group was large enough to avoid awkward pauses in conversation, in truth it had more to do with my lingering irritation at Richard for not bailing me out of the poker game. Although, to be fair, that experience had proved to be an inspiration for my writing.

Myrtle arrived first, a good ten minutes before the time I'd told her. She locked in on Richard at once, which is something I've been watching women do for over forty years. Although he normally revels in such attention and occasionally exploits it, I could see this time he was relieved when the doorbell rang and Edna arrived, followed closely by Norman.

Five minutes after that, Josephine and Lillian arrived, and the living room filled with a steady hum of conversation. I tried not to interfere with that as I passed the hors d'oeuvres—mini quiches and a selection of decadent deep-fried bits of cheese, mushroom, and for the health conscious, zucchini.

Richard was eating more of the bits than he should, but there was no way I could stop him short of moving the plates farther away. Which I did. Myrtle, telling me how delicious everything was, changed seats to remain close to the food. I caught Josephine's eye, and she winked at me.

Seeing the level in some glasses going down, I went to the kitchen to open another bottle of wine.

Norman followed me. "I've been wanting to talk to you," he said. "But I rarely see you."

"I've been hiding out. I'm working on a new book, you see." I gestured at the glass he was holding, and when he nodded, I got another bottle of wine from the refrigerator and opened it.

I poured more wine into his glass. "What did you want to talk about?"

"About what Myrtle said the other day. You know, while we were playing poker?"

"You mean about the painting, right? I checked, and I doubt she knew what she was talking about. An Edward Hopper painting could be worth as much as forty million dollars. I bet she made it up, just like she did that bit about Edna stealing her sister's fiancé, or her being in the finals of the Miss Ohio pageant."

"You think those stories are fictional?"

"Don't you?" I leaned back against the counter.

"Not necessarily." He took a sip of wine, looking thoughtful. "After all, Edna did admit she did what Myrtle accused her of."

"So you believe there was an Edward Hopper painting. Here at Brookside?"

"When you say it like that, it seems unlikely."

"Why don't you just ask Josephine?"

"I already have."

"And?"

Norman frowned. "She changed the subject."

"So we're talking major mystery here? Hmm. Maybe Brookside is going to be more interesting than I expected."

The two of us rejoined the group in the living room, and I refilled other glasses.

"I have a question for you." Josephine directed the comment to Norman, who had taken a seat near Richard. "What do you know about cons and con artists?"

"I'm not sure what you mean."

"As a forensic accountant, you must have encountered all sorts of diddles. What I'm most interested in is cons or scams that target the elderly."

"I see what you mean."

"I wondered if you have any thoughts about how to prevent them?"

"I haven't given it much thought." Norman cocked his head and examined Josephine.

"Has someone tried to con you?" I asked, giving Richard a sideways glance. He raised his hands in a *don't look at me, I'm innocent* gesture.

She shook her head. "And it's not just scams we need to protect ourselves from. We also need protection from being declared incompetent so a relative can take over our affairs."

"Someone can do that?" Myrtle sounded shocked.

"Certainly," Josephine said. "There was a case recently. In Seattle, I believe. A woman who was doing fine on her own until someone who wasn't even a family member got himself appointed her guardian. He cleaned out her accounts with bogus charges and left her nearly penniless."

"You're right," Norman said. "I saw a report about that case."

"Here in Ohio, protective services can step in and ask the courts for guardianship," I said. "Then the person's resources are transferred to the state."

"You sound like you have experience in that regard," Norman said making a question of it.

"In a former life, I was an attorney. Family law."

"How interesting." Myrtle had her hand on her throat, and the words sounded breathless.

"Nothing makes me madder than people who prey on others they view as weak and vulnerable. Legally or illegally." Although Josephine hadn't raised her voice, there was passion fueling the words.

"Well, Josephine may not have been conned, but I almost was." Myrtle obviously relished the shift of attention as we all turned to look at her. "I got a phone call from someone who pretended to be my granddaughter. She claimed she'd been arrested in Mexico and needed money to pay her fine so she could get out of jail. And I was all ready to send her everything she asked for. But since I had no idea what a green card thingy was to transfer the money, I asked Lillian about it, and she got Josephine involved."

Edna eyes widened. "What happened then?"

"Josephine made me realize I'd jumped to the conclusion the caller was Stephanie and used that name first. And then I'd given her other clues, like wasn't she supposed to be in school, and had she called her parents. That gave the caller all the information she needed to convince me she was Stephanie and desperately in need of money."

"But it could have been Stephanie," Edna insisted.

"It wasn't. Josephine had me call Stephanie, and she was right where she was supposed to be. At school, studying."

"There are other variations," Norman said. "Someone poses as an old friend, e-mails you, and says they're overseas somewhere and have lost their wallet and passport and can you send money."

"An e-mail con isn't going to be very successful here," Lillian said. "Only a few of us use computers. And besides, most of my friends are too old to gallivant around the world, dribbling passports hither and yon."

"What about sweepstakes?" Josephine said.

"All you have to do is pay a small administrative fee or, even better, provide your bank account number so the money can get to you as soon as possible," Norman responded.

"If it seems too good to be true...," Josephine said.

"It probably isn't. True, that is," Norman finished.

The two exchanged a satisfied look.

Clearly, my party was a success. I passed around more fried bits, but shortly after that, Myrtle heaved herself to her feet saying it was time for dinner. That broke up the party.

"Well," Richard said as the last guest left, "that had its interesting moments."

"It did. And I hope you'll agree that I can get back to my book now?"

"Just glad to see you're making an effort, love." He kissed me and then helped pick up the plates and glasses.

He always has been a most thoughtful husband, and I love him dearly, even if being married to him meant I had to retire before I was ready. And move to Brookside.

Chapter Thirteen

Devi

The first week of February, I drove to the Cincinnati Art Museum where I spent the morning filling out forms, getting badges and keys, and settling into my office.

In the afternoon, Miriam O'Pinsky showed up to give me a tour. Until Josephine offered me the position, I hadn't visited the museum, knowing it would have been a sad reminder of all I'd had to give up in Chicago. But since New Year's, I'd visited twice. That didn't mean I wasn't excited about the opportunity to have Miriam show me around, particularly behind the scenes.

"One of the things I want to do is go over our security measures," Miriam said. "I'm certain Josephine will want your opinion of them. By the way, have you seen it? *Sea Watchers*, that is?"

I nodded. "It's spectacular. It was one of my favorites of his, even before I saw it in person."

"And Josephine just had it hanging in her apartment?"

"It was safe when nobody knew she had it. I think most people would have assumed it was a copy."

"So, what happened?"

"Her son spotted it. Figured out it was the real deal and made a huge fuss. Almost got it stolen as a result." I decided I wouldn't tell Miriam the whole story—the part about Josephine and her son being estranged.

"Where's the painting now?"

"I know only generalities, not specifics. We all think that's best, for the time being."

"Yes, I expect you're right. Well, here's where we'll hang it."

We had entered a large square gallery lit by lights recessed behind panels high in the ceiling. My eyes were drawn to the museum's current Hopper painting, *Sun on Prospect Street,* and the space next to it, which was blank. *Sea Watchers* will be a nice contrast, since it has human figures and *Sun on Prospect Street* doesn't.

I turned in a circle, noting that the two Hoppers would be focal points as visitors entered the gallery.

"I think Josephine will approve," I told Miriam.

She smiled, looking relieved.

"What was here before?"

"As a matter of fact, the Grant Wood painting we loaned to the Winterford. By the time it returned, I thought of this as my wishing spot."

"Wishing spot?"

"A place where I could dream about possibilities. I wanted to leave it bare in order to summon something wonderful. And now it has. *Sea Watchers...*it's so much more than I thought might be possible." She stopped speaking, and after a moment, cleared her throat. "Okay. Security measures. For starters, whenever the museum is open, at least one of our guards will be present in this area or close by."

She proceeded to point out the location of the cameras and motion sensors that covered the approaches to the gallery, and were set high enough to defy efforts to blank them with spray paint.

"How long before you're ready to exhibit the painting?" I asked when we returned to her office.

"Maybe April? That will give us plenty of time to plan its debut."

"What are your thoughts about that?"

"We'll want to throw a party for our major donors and members, and invite all the media and...And I think the planning for that could be your first assignment."

Although tired by the end of the day and still worried about the situation with Mac and Lisa, I floated out to my car for the commute home feeling, at least professionally, I was back where I belonged.

Chapter Fourteen

Josephine

I invited Devi for lunch on Saturday to find out how her first week at the museum had gone. She arrived smiling and full of excitement.

"Miriam said you can place *Sea Watchers* in their keeping whenever you're ready, and I'm to plan the special events for when the painting goes on display."

"I suppose it would be a good idea to move it to the museum."

"Yes, I think so. Too many people know about it. And even though you and Mac are keeping mum about where you stashed it, well, for forty million dollars, it would be worth someone's time to work out where that is."

"Speaking of Mac, how is he? I haven't seen him since you two came to dinner on New Year's."

She shifted and bit her lip. "He's..." She stopped and closed her eyes, and I felt a swoop of dismay. I'd been so sure about them. As had Lill, after she did the couples analysis of their handwriting samples.

"What is it?" I reached out to touch her hand. I don't know why, but Devi taps into my maternal instincts in a way my son hasn't since he was five.

"It's just...It's his ex-wife. She's staying with him. And she's pregnant."

Startled, I sat blinking at her. It was the last thing I expected her to say about Mac. "Well..." But after that one word, I couldn't come up with anything further.

"It's not what you're thinking, though. He's not the father, and they're not reconciling. She needed a temporary place to stay, and Mac didn't feel he could say no. She was only supposed to stay a few days, but now..."

Devi then brought me up to date on morals clauses in Cincinnati Catholic school contracts.

"But that's barbaric."

"That's one thing we all agree on. Not that it helps the current situation. Because of it, Lisa told the principal she and Mac remarried."

"Oh. That isn't—"

"Good? No, it isn't. I invited him to live with me, but he said didn't want to start our life together that way. And that leaves us stuck."

"But he's talking about a life with you? You realize that's huge?"

She nodded.

"Can Mac afford to move to another place?"

She shook her head. "He's still paying off his part of the cost of the fertility treatments. He's pretty strapped."

Going into debt to conceive a baby was one dilemma my generation hadn't needed to worry about.

"And he won't accept any help from me, in case you're wondering," Devi added. "We already talked about it. Turns out he's also old-fashioned about money."

"More than you'd like him to be?"

She sighed. "Not really. It's part of what makes him who he is. So if I ask him to change that..."

"I see your difficulty." For my generation, putting off things like sex and marriage or having babies until we could afford it came as part of the package, but looking at the modern world, I knew such considerations were no longer the given they used to be.

Devi sighed again. "Guess I just have to resign myself to a long courtship."

"That's not all bad, you know."

"I know. Mac and I are still getting to know each other, and although I'm certain we'll end up together, I'm okay with taking it slow."

"Good. Glad to hear it. I think Mac is worth waiting for."

Devi smiled. "Oh yes. I think so too."

Chapter Fifteen

Mac

Josephine called in early February to ask for my help in transferring the Hopper painting from the storage unit where we'd taken it in December to the Cincinnati Art Museum.

I was glad to hear it was moving to a more secure location. Having a painting worth possibly as much as forty million just sitting in a storage unit with no particular security had never been the best idea. At least, not for long.

On my next day off, I arrived at Brookside at ten a.m. as requested to find Josephine standing by the back door, ready to go. Since we'd avoided rush hour, we managed the trip to the storage unit and from there to the museum in less than an hour.

The parking lot attendant at the museum directed us to a side entrance used for deliveries, and the museum's director, Miriam O'Pinsky, met us there along with Devi and two guards. I smiled at Devi, delighted as always to see her, before walking around to open the tailgate of my SUV.

The two guards stepped forward and, together, they carried the painting inside, handling it with great formality. Miriam told me I could leave my vehicle where it was, so I took up my position at the back of the procession.

After reaching the designated location in the basement storage area, one of the guards unveiled the painting, and we all stood looking at it in silence. Now that I knew how much it was worth, I looked more intently than I had before, and I could see what Devi meant when she said that Hopper managed to capture the essential loneliness that's inside each of us. In Josephine's painting, a man and a woman sit beside each other on a bench outside a beach shack, and although they're physically close, the emotional gulf between them is obvious.

Looking at the painting produced a visceral memory of how far apart Lisa and I had been by the time our marriage ended. And it made me resolve never to let that happen with Devi.

After we'd had our fill of staring at the painting, Miriam invited Josephine upstairs to see the spot where they planned to hang *Sea Watchers*. Devi and I followed, but while Josephine and Miriam went into the gallery, we stood together overlooking the rotunda.

I took Devi's hand in mine because I love touching her and then I looked around. From our vantage point, I could see several paintings and sculptures.

"We couldn't have two more different professions," I told Devi.

"What do you mean?"

I gestured toward the nearest painting. "You focus your efforts to preserve and display the fruits of mankind's better side—the part of us that creates beautiful things that endure. I'm more likely to be dealing with what comes from our dark side."

"Then it can't hurt to be reminded there is a better side."

"I'm reminded of that every time I'm with you," I said.

Her startled expression made me realize I rarely told her, or anyone, what they meant to me, and I vowed to do better. However, I lost my chance to do that in the present moment when Miriam and Josephine rejoined us. After telling us good-bye, Miriam left us, and Devi led the way back to where I'd left my vehicle.

As I pulled into the parking lot at Brookside, Josephine put her hand on my arm. "I wonder if I can impose on you for one more thing, Mac."

"Of course. You know you can."

"I do know that, and I hope you realize what a blessing I consider it to be."

Her choice of words surprised me. Josephine isn't into religion any more than I am. When we prayed for Devi in the hospital, it was Lillian who addressed the Almighty. All Josephine and I pitched in were the heartfelt amens.

"If you wouldn't mind coming in for a minute?"

I nodded, turned the engine off, and got out to open her door, although, being Josephine, she'd hopped out by the time I got there. She led the way into her apartment and gestured for me to take a seat on the sofa.

"I need to ask you a huge favor." She stopped talking and chewed on her lip.

I waited.

"I trust you." Again she paused. "And I want you to be my health-care proxy and to have my durable power of attorney."

"Don't you want Devi to do that for you?"

"No. I trust you both, but the reason I'm not asking Devi is because I'm her employer, and I don't intend to give my son any room to either challenge my wishes or to circumvent them. I believe there's no better way to avoid that than you, Darren McElroy."

"I-I'm honored."

"You're willing, then?"

"Yes. I am." But I hoped it wouldn't be an issue for a long time to come.

"Good. It may not be an easy assignment, you know. I doubt my son will give up after only one attempt."

Josephine was referring to the time her son had her admitted to a psychiatric facility as a first step toward having her declared incompetent to manage her own affairs. Dillingham and I had rescued her.

"Just let him try," I said.

"Thank you, Mac. I'll get the paperwork started."

She stood and so did I, thinking our meeting was over. But then she opened the closet door and pointed at a box that was sitting there. "I wanted to give you this for Christmas. But it took longer to arrive than I expected."

She gestured for me to slide the box out. It was heavy and had a complex shipping label attached. The printing on the side of the box read Erdradour Distillery, Pitlochry, Scotland. I looked at Josephine to find her grinning at me.

"I couldn't get a full case of thirty-year-old Scotch," she said. "So I had them add a couple of bottles that were fifty years old instead."

I gulped. The box I had so nonchalantly pulled from her closet contained several thousand dollars' worth of elderly Scotch, and although I knew Josephine could afford it, her generosity still overwhelmed me.

She waved a hand at me. "No. I don't want to hear a thing about it being too much. Being able to live free of my son's interference is worth much more to me than a few bottles of Scotch. And it won't hurt my feelings, by the way, if you auction off some of it."

I straightened and looked her in the eye. She looked right back, her expression bland. Then she shook her head. "Not one word. Just take it. And enjoy."

I shook my head. "I wish I could. But we have rules about accepting gifts."

"Okay, how's this? Darren McElroy, I need your help to deliver this case of Scotch to Devi Subramanian. It's her Christmas gift."

"Josephine..."

"Either you take it now, or I'll hire someone to deliver it later."

I took it.

Chapter Sixteen

Josephine

For the third time in a week, I found a message from my son, Jeff, on my answering device.

"Mother, we should talk. I hate that you're angry with me. Yeah, I know. I screwed up. But I'm really, really sorry. I promise I'll do better if you give me another chance. We're family, after all. But, anyway...call me."

With each ensuing message, although his words sounded conciliatory, his tone was becoming increasingly belligerent. But, after all, I'd been an irritation to him most of his life so why would I expect that to change? A relief to know Mac would shortly be in a legal position to watch my back.

Like Jeff's other messages, I deleted it.

~ ~ ~

Norman forced himself on Lill and me at dinner a second time.

"I thought we might discuss doing a workshop on the scams and cons we talked about at Philippa's," he said as he sat down.

"What an excellent idea," Lill said. "You know, I was just reading about a new scam."

"What's that?" I'd greeted Norman, but then, signaling my displeasure at his presence, I returned my attention to Lill.

"You get a call saying that since you failed to report for jury duty, you now owe a thousand-dollar fine," Lill said. "And if you don't pay immediately, you'll be held in contempt of court and put in jail. Doctors and lawyers are falling for it. They're so busy, they assume they overlooked the summons. The scammers even use the names of real people involved in the courts."

"Seems like predators suffer no lack of imagination," I said. "It's just too bad they don't use that creativity in a more positive way."

"Amen to that," Lill said.

Reluctantly, I turned to Norman. "You know, a workshop probably is a good idea."

"How do you suggest we get started?" Norman asked after the waitress delivered our salads and took our orders.

"We could do skits," Lill said.

Fork suspended, I thought about it. "You know, that's an excellent idea. It may stick with people much longer than if we do a talk."

"We should prepare a handout to go with it," Norman said.

I nodded. "Yes. I agree. Why don't I do a draft and you can add to it? And then we'll figure out the skits and recruit our actors."

"I bet Myrtle will be first in line," Lill said with a chuckle.

"At least she won't get stage fright."

Chapter Seventeen

Lillian

I was excited by the discussion at dinner with Norman and Josephine. No one ever asked the math teacher to help with school theatrical productions, but I would have liked to do it. How funny it took my moving into a retirement community near the end of my life to fulfill a dream I didn't even know I had.

"How about this, Josephine?" I said after the two of us returned to her apartment following dinner. "You and Norman write the scripts, and I'll recruit actors and direct?"

"Must we involve Norman that much?" Josephine responded.

"He's the one pushing the idea. And he'll not only be a good addition, working together will give you a chance to get to know him better."

"I don't want to get to know him better. Philippa can help with the scripts. After all, she's a writer."

"That's a great idea. We can work in teams. You and Norman suggest the cons and scams and prepare the handout. Philippa and I will work on scripts and actors."

"You're relentless, you know that?"

"That's what my Roger always said. Called me Relly for short."

Josephine shook her head and barely suppressed an eye roll.

"You'll see. It'll be fun. We get it organized, we might even go on the road."

"What do you mean, go on the road?" Josephine said.

"Why visit other retirement communities. This could be huge."

"Well, don't buy a dress for the Oscars just yet."

"You mean Tonys."

"Tonys?"

"Aren't they the awards for live theater? You'll see. This will be so much fun."

"I suppose it could be interesting," Josephine conceded.

"Let's talk to Philippa tomorrow. Then we can tell Norman what we've decided."

This time Josephine did roll her eyes. But I knew I was on to something, and I wasn't letting her lack of enthusiasm stop me.

Chapter Eighteen

Mac

"I've decided to move," Devi told me on Valentine's Day. She'd fixed dinner, and we planned a quiet evening at her apartment.

Since I'd spent freely on takeout dinners when she was first home from the hospital, and my budget was staggering because of it, I was happy for the change to home-cooked meals. That didn't mean I didn't feel guilty about not making more of a fuss over Valentine's. But the day held unpleasant associations for both Devi and me—she of her engagement, me of Lisa's celebratory requirements—and together we'd decided to ignore the commercial pressure to do more than spend the evening together.

"Why move?" I asked her. "I thought you said this place suited you."

"Here's the thing. Miriam knows a faculty member at the University of Cincinnati who's going on sabbatical in a couple of months. He and his wife have a house in Montgomery, and they want someone to live there while they're away. They'll be gone a year."

She stopped speaking, and I knew it was in order for me to ask questions, but I wasn't sure what they should be.

"I met them and checked out the house today. It has five bedrooms and a mother-in-law suite."

"How much is the rent?"

"It's house-sitting, not renting. They have a dog and a couple of cats, you see. And I'd have to take care of arranging any repairs. There's gardening in the spring, and—"

"What about this apartment? Don't you have a lease?"

"It's almost up, and you don't have a lease, right?"

"No. I go from month to month, in case the house sells. And it probably will in the spring."

She pulled in a deep breath that made her wince and press on her side, something that always makes me wince too.

"So...here's what I'm thinking. You give up your house, Lisa moves in here and takes over my lease, and the two of us house-sit for a year. There's plenty of room. The house is huge. I'll take the mother-in-law suite and you can pick whatever bedroom you like, and you can help with the outside work, and—"

"Whoa. Slow down. Take a breath. This needs to be thought out. For one thing, is this couple going to like the idea of me moving in if their agreement is with you?" Too late, I realized I'd all but accepted her plan. But then, it was a pretty good one.

"I already asked them. They both thought having a Montgomery police detective living in their house was a terrific idea. Although they did say they'd like to meet you. But I think they just want to make sure the dog likes you."

"Did it like you?"

She nodded, smiling. "It's some kind of terrier named Tuckie, and it's a terror, but yes, it did like me, and they said it doesn't take to very many people."

"So I'd have to pass the Tuckie terror-terrier test." My tongue stumbled on the words and Devi grinned.

"You would. What do you think? Is it a good idea?"

"Everything except maybe the part about moving Lisa into this apartment."

"You do admit though, she's not doing anything to find another place."

I shook my head in frustration at Lisa's continuing inaction on the housing front. I'd given up nudging her about it a couple of weeks earlier after it resulted in an angry exchange that reminded me too clearly of why we'd ended up divorced. Short of physically moving her stuff to the curb and changing the locks, I'd come to the conclusion I was stuck for the duration.

It was also now clear that had been Lisa's intention all along, and I wanted to kick myself for not realizing it sooner. Still, I didn't see how I could have acted differently that first night.

"When do these people want to meet me?" I asked.

"Tomorrow. You're off at five, right? I can meet you at the safety center, and we can go together."

"Sounds like a plan."

She smiled, obviously relieved. "It does, doesn't it."

~ ~ ~

"Mrs. Livingston, this is Detective Darren McElroy. Mac, Janet Livingston."

I shook the woman's hand and greeted her, or tried to, but a small dog had materialized behind her and was dancing about barking so madly, we ended up just smiling at each other. Meanwhile, Devi bent over and held out a dog treat. Tuckie stopped barking, moved closer, and sniffed. Behind her back, she handed me a second treat.

Following her lead, I sat on my haunches and held the treat within reach, but without moving my hand toward the dog. It grabbed the treat from Devi and backed away, chewing and eyeing the two of us with apparently deep suspicion. After gulping down Devi's offering, Tuckie stretched his neck to get closer to the treat I was holding without actually moving toward me.

I waited, and after an interval of careful sniffing, he skittered close enough to pull the treat from my hand. Then he jumped away, and holding it in his mouth, sidled over to Devi as if to let me know she was under his protection. Chuckling, I stood to find Janet Livingston smiling.

"It appears you've also earned the Tuckie stamp of approval, Detective."

"Please, call me Mac."

"Mac." She smiled at me. "It suits you. And I'm Janet."

She took us on a tour, introducing us to her husband along the way. The house, one of the large homes built on the border between Montgomery and Indian Hill and less than a mile from the Montgomery Safety Center where I work, was impressive.

Devi and I could live together in this house and rarely see each other, if that was what we wanted, since the mother-in-law suite had its own kitchen and was larger than Devi's current apartment. Living here, we could work on our relationship without the pressure of a premature joining of households.

"And there's plenty of space in the garage if you need to store any of your things," Janet said, concluding the tour.

"Did you want us to sign an agreement?" Devi asked as we took seats in the family room.

"Oh, I've checked on the two of you. I spoke with your boss." She nodded at me. "He couldn't have recommended you more highly. As for you, Devi, Miriam spoke in glowing terms. And last, but not least, Tuckie approves of you both." The small dog had followed us as we took the tour and was now snoozing on Janet's lap.

We talked about logistics and arrangements. Janet was hoping Devi would move in at least a week before they left, so Tuckie could better accept their departure.

"Actually, the sooner you move in, the better, although I expect you have arrangements to make. But if you're here ahead of time, it'll give us a chance to make sure you know everything you'll need to know. Of course, we'll be in touch by e-mail and phone while we're away. Still, it's better if we show you how everything works. Just name the day. Oh, and let me give you both keys."

"What did you think?" Devi said as we drove back to the safety center to pick up my vehicle.

"I didn't know college professors could afford houses like that."

"I thought the same thing, but I couldn't very well ask about it."

"Maybe there's family money."

"Maybe. It is a terrific house. It'll be fun living there."

"We just better not get too accustomed to it."

Devi shuddered. "Oh, I'd never want to live in a house that grand for real."

Which was a relief, because I was never going to be able to afford a house like that. Not even close.

Chapter Nineteen

Josephine

When I arrived in the dining room for lunch, Lill waved me over to where she was sitting with Norman and Philippa.

"I've told them what we discussed about the workshop," Lill said.

"And I'm in," Philippa said. "I think you're right about the skits being the most effective way to present the information. And I'll be happy to write them for you."

"You can get Norman to help you." I glanced at him, moving my foot out of Lill's reach just in time. "He can give you the details about how the scams work. Right?" I looked at Norman.

"Sure, sounds good," he said.

"We've been talking about which ones to focus on," Philippa said. "We think the 'grandchild in trouble' is the most important one, and then we can do an IRS scam and the 'you've missed jury duty' one. So that's three at least."

"What about a sweepstakes skit?"

"Hmm. Lots of possible variations there." She paused, chewing on her lip. "I can give it a try."

"So it seems the first step is for you to work with Nori on the details and then write the dialogue. As soon as you finish the skits, Lill will find people to fill the parts, and she can rehearse them. Finally, I'll start working on the handout."

"I think you need to work with Norman on the handout," Lill said.

The temptation to give her a kick was overwhelming.

"Seems we have a plan," Norman said. "You know," he turned to me, "if you sit in while Philippa and I talk about the skits, that should help with the handout."

"In that case, Lill might as well join us so she can begin thinking about who to ask to be in the skits," I said.

"We could have our first meeting after lunch," Philippa said. "Why don't we meet at my place. Oops, I forgot. Richard is having a friend over. How about we meet at your place, Josephine?"

With a flash of annoyance, I wondered if Philippa was in cahoots with Lill, trying to throw me together with Norman. Well, it wasn't going to work.

"I'm sorry," I said. "The plumber's coming for a...a sink stoppage. Maybe we could meet in the library? It's usually deserted after lunch." I glanced at Norman to find him examining me as intently as Mac does when he suspects me of planning something nefarious.

~ ~ ~

With Lill so determined to throw me under the Norman bus, I decided I needed to know more about him. So after our workshop meeting, I called the investigator recommended by my lawyer.

"What sort of information are you trying to find?" the investigator said. "This man isn't a relative, is he?"

"No. He's not. Mainly, I'm interested in his work history. He claims to have been a forensic accountant."

"You doubt that?"

"Not necessarily. I'd just like to know exactly what I'm dealing with. How soon can you get me a report?"

"Depends on whether he told you the truth, and whether he's using his real name."

"Sooner rather than later would be most appreciated."

The investigator called three days later with a full report, and what he'd discovered about Norman was well worth the substantial fee he charged.

Chapter Twenty

Mac

Although I'd been avoiding Lisa as much as possible, that was more difficult to do when my days off fell on the weekend. The Saturday after Devi and I went to look at the Livingstons' house, I walked into the kitchen and noticed how rounded Lisa's stomach was becoming. She was seven months along, but to my admittedly unpracticed eye, she looked more pregnant than that.

I set the basket of dirty laundry on the floor and turned away from her to sort towels from shirts. "How are you feeling?"

"Fat. And my back's been killing me."

"Isn't it too soon for that?"

"Not when you're carrying twins."

I dropped a towel and turned to face her. "What?"

"You heard me. I'm carrying twins."

"How long have you known?"

She shrugged. "Since my first sonogram."

"And you didn't think to mention it because...?"

"I think I did."

"No. You didn't."

It was typical Lisa behavior. She loved to know things nobody else knew.

I'd been working hard to think of her pregnancy as only an inconvenience. But twins. Good Lord. That doubled, maybe more, the chance of something going wrong. I knew that because we'd both read about multiple births before starting down the embryo-implantation road. I was still paying my share of the last procedure where we'd opted for two embryos to be implanted.

And what about the irony in the current situation? Unable to get pregnant while married to me, even with all the assistance that modern medicine had to offer, then she had a brief fling with someone else and ended up pregnant. With twins. Further proof, not that I needed it, the creator of the universe has one weird sense of humor.

Twins also meant keeping her medical insurance was even more critical. And that would be problematic if someone figured out she wasn't married.

With a start, I realized what I was seeing. A wedding ring on the third finger of the hand she had wrapped around a mug of coffee. The sight made me profoundly uneasy. All it would take was one busybody and a Google search to blow her cover. Although saying we remarried in Mexico might help obscure the truth.

"So, Darren? Aren't you spending the day with the girlfriend?"

Without answering, I turned back to my laundry and measured out detergent.

"You do realize if someone who knows us both sees you with her, it could cause me a major problem."

I whirled to face her. "It's not enough you move in here, lying about needing a place to stay for a *few* days, now you're dictating how I'm allowed to conduct my personal life?"

"Is she pretty?"

"She's gorgeous. Inside and out."

Her eyes widened, and I realized I'd intended the words as a rebuke, and she knew it.

"Well, lucky you."

I turned back to the washer, closed the lid, and took a breath. I needed to get away from Lisa. Not just today, but permanently.

And a thought about how to do that required only a nanosecond. As soon as Devi moved to the Livingstons', I'd move into her apartment and stay there until the day I could also move to the Livingstons'.

But I'd wait to tell Lisa until it was a fait accompli.

I started the washer, put on my outdoor clothes, then walked next door to offer to take Teddy and Bruno for a walk. Teddy is a five-year-old with Down Syndrome, and Bruno's a hound of some sort that has too much dignity to prance around barking his head off like Tuckie.

Bruno helped to save Devi's life by pushing between her and the gunman and then knocking Devi to the ground and lying on top of her. Because the bullet hit Bruno first, it hadn't done as much damage to Devi as it could have.

Still, it was a near thing for both of them. Bruno also needed surgery afterward, but like Devi, he seems to have mostly bounced back, and both he and Teddy love to walk, no matter how cold it is. As for me, I find walking with the two of them is one way to get my priorities realigned and my thinking straight.

By the time I returned to my house, I was calm again. But I was still glad to discover that Lisa had gone out.

Chapter Twenty-One

Devi

Saturday morning, shortly after I returned from running errands, there was a knock on the door. I almost didn't answer. When I'm not expecting someone, I ignore people at my door the same way I avoid unknown callers on my phone.

But then, thinking it could be Mac, although he wasn't due until lunchtime, I answered the door to find a very pregnant very blonde woman on my doorstep.

"Lisa McElroy." She extended a hand that I shook reluctantly. "I believe you're acquainted with my husband, Darren? Can I come in?"

I stood aside, and she walked past me, her head swiveling as she looked around. It didn't swivel long as there was little to see. She walked over to my kitchen table and sat in one of the two chairs and then gave me a look that commanded me to take the other chair. Mac had told me she was a teacher. Based on the power of that look, I suspected her students behaved.

"My goodness. Are you even legal?"

Since I'm frequently told I look much younger than my thirty-two years, the comment didn't throw me the way I was sure she'd hoped it would. Although, I suppose she could have been referring instead to the fact I resemble my Indian father.

I gave her a look of my own. "What is it you want?"

"Just checking out my husband's...extracurriculars." She gave me an arch look, rested her elbows on the table, and played with the ring on the third finger of her left hand. "You're satisfied with being the *other* woman, are you? You do know he's terribly messy?" She glanced around. "I can see you're not, and once the initial glow wears off, I think that might get to you. Dirty dishes in the sink. Clothing scattered from the front door to the bedroom. Beer bottles leaving rings on your furniture. Not that your things are nice enough for that to be a worry."

After being shot and almost dying, my perceptions have undergone a change. I knew she was goading me, but instead of seeing the threat in her words, I saw their essential desperation.

"He prefers blondes, you know." She tossed her head and ran the hand with the ring on it through her hair. "When he strayed before, it was always with a blonde. I forgive him, you know." She leaned toward me. "He's no great shakes; let me be the first to assure you of that. He snores, and tosses and turns."

Having slept in Mac's arms, I knew that wasn't true.

"And frankly, he's not a very good lover. But you must know that. And he never remembers birthdays or anniversaries. But the main thing about him is he's mine."

I'd sometimes worried, when I awoke in the middle of the night and couldn't get back to sleep, that Mac might want to find a way to break it off with me so he could have a family with Lisa. But the more Lisa talked, the more convinced I was that Mac wasn't hedging the truth when he said he felt an obligation to help her, but otherwise didn't want any part of this woman.

"What's wrong with you, cat got your tongue? Or maybe you don't even speak English, huh?"

"What do you want me to say?"

"Nothing. Just remind Darren he has a pregnant wife who needs him."

I nodded, then I stood, and after a pause, she stood too. I walked her to the door and reached around her to open it.

She turned in the doorway. "You tell him what I said, you hear me." With a final glare that encompassed both me and my apartment, she turned and stalked out.

Breathing a sigh of relief, I made sure I locked the door. Then, hands shaking, I made myself a cup of tea and sat sipping it.

When Mac showed up an hour later, I debated whether to tell him about Lisa's visit. On the one hand I didn't want to burden him, but on the other, since I wanted him to share his life with me, I knew I needed to do the same.

While he helped me prepare grilled cheese sandwiches and tomato soup for our lunch, he talked about taking Teddy and Bruno for a walk.

I waited until we started to eat to tell him my news. "Lisa came to see me this morning."

His head snapped up, and he stared at me with that careful assessing *cop* look of his. Then he blinked in apparent confusion. "I never told her your name or where you lived."

"I didn't ask how she found me. Maybe she followed you?"

He rubbed his forehead. "That could be. What did she want?"

"She claimed to be married to you. Called me the other woman. Said you'd strayed before, but you preferred blondes. That she always forgives you, and that even though you aren't any great shakes as a husband, you're hers."

He sat back blinking and fiddling with his knife. "Wow. What did you say?"

"I told her I'd speak to you and remind you, you have a wife with a baby on the way."

"Two babies."

"What?"

"She told me this morning. She's carrying twins."

"Wow. She really is a regular Mary Sunshine."

"You do know she's lying about being married to me?"

"I know you're divorced. Josephine checked."

"Oh, she did, did she?"

"Before she turned over several thousand dollars' worth of Scotch, she wanted to be sure your intentions toward me were honorable."

"Well, if they're not, I'd be out of luck since you've got the Scotch."

"Yes, you would."

"And just so you know, I never cheated on her."

I reached across the space between us and took one of his hands in mine.

"I do know that. You may just be the most honorable person I know, besides Josephine."

"Glad to hear I'm in good company on that." He looked down at our hands. "When Lisa told me about the twins...I decided I had to get away from her as soon as possible. I thought, if it's all right with you, I'll move in here when you move to the Livingstons'."

"I called Janet after Lisa left. She said I can move in tomorrow. Which means you have only tonight to get through, and you can spend that on my couch, if you like." I paused and took a calming breath. "When you do see Lisa, don't say anything about her coming to see me, okay?"

"Any particular reason?"

"She's playing the role of the aggrieved wife to the hilt. You don't need to give her any more ammunition."

"I expect you're right. The less I talk to Lisa, the better it is all around."

~ ~ ~

"Now," Lillian said, "this is just like playing poker. You have a great hand, but your job is not to give anything away while getting all the information you need from Myrtle so you can convince her you're her granddaughter."

"In a word, I'm conning her." It wasn't the help I was expecting to provide. I thought Josephine and Lillian wanted me to assist with general logistics for the workshop, because Norman's new and Candace, who is the actual activities director, never seems to do much.

"Precisely. You're conning her. Now, Philippa has written a script, so why don't we start with you practicing that with Myrtle?"

"Sure. Just give me a minute to take a look." I glanced through the two pages and then turned back to the first page. "What is it you want me to say here?" I pointed at the first word on the page.

"Oh, that," Philippa said. "You need to do a mix of granny and nanna."

"Granna?"

"Good, only spread it out and make it sound as panicked and indistinct as you can."

"Graaaaan...a."

"Very good. What do you think, Myrtle?"

"It's eerie. That's exactly what she sounded like."

"She?"

"Didn't you know? This skit is based on a call I received. And I very nearly fell for it."

"Shall we try it then?" Lillian said. "Devi, you could pretend you're talking into your phone. And Myrtle will answer on her phone."

Myrtle, at the other end of the table, was sitting queen-like beside a pink princess phone. I wondered how she'd know to answer it as she has a tendency to be literal, but I need not have worried. Josephine held a recorder in her hand and when she clicked it on, it made the sound of a ringing phone. Lillian gestured to Myrtle, who picked up the handset and said hello.

"Graaaan—"

"Hello, hello? Stephanie? Nicole? Anita, is that you? Is something wrong?"

"Oh, Graaan, it's Stephanie. I'm in terrible trouble."

"What's happened? Aren't you studying for finals?"

"No, no. I was. I mean, finals are done. And friends talked me into going t-to Mexico to celebrate." Throughout, I kept that thread of panic in my voice. "And now I'm in an awful mess."

"Have you called your dad?"

"N-no. I can't call him. He'd be so—"

"Of course. He'd be very upset. What about your mom?"

"You know how she is. If she knew they arrested me, she'd freak out. You're the only one I can ask for help."

"Arrested? Darling Stephie, what can I do to help? You know I can't come to Mexico. Do you need money?"

"No, no. Of course you can't come. But they took my money, and I need to pay the fine and it's so scary here. And dirty. Can't you please, please help me?"

"Oh, Stephie, you know I will. How much do you need?"

"T-two thousand."

"Two thousand. Okay."

"That's for the fine. I'll need another thousand so I can get home. I'm so scared."

"Now, Stephanie, you know your gran will do whatever I can to help you, sweetie."

"Would you, Gran? You're the best. All you need to do is buy three thousand dollars' worth of green-dot cards. Then you call and give me the numbers of the cards so the money can be transferred."

"Okay. Let me just write this all down."

"They took my phone, so I have to give you the number to call once you have the cards."

"Okay." Myrtle juggled the phone and a pen.

Clearly, in real life, managing to write down the information correctly would be a challenge for Myrtle. I went off script, saying, "Are you ready, Gran?"

"Yes, yes, of course." Myrtle sounded flustered, which I thought was perfect for her part. "That wasn't in the script, you know." She finally snugged the phone with her shoulder and was holding the pen, ready to write.

"Devi's right, though," Philippa said. "I'll get that added."

I recited the phone number in the script, speaking slowly while Myrtle wrote. Then Lillian stepped up to the table where Myrtle and I were sitting.

She smiled and gave us a thumbs-up. "You both did great. What we're thinking is we'll stop here and ask our audience if they have any suggestions to offer Myrtle."

I could think of several. "Did you really think it was your granddaughter?" I asked Myrtle.

"I'm afraid I did. But lucky for me, I asked Lillian for help with the green thingy-bobby cards they told me to use, and she told Josephine. And Josephine called Stephanie and proved she was right where she was supposed to be. At college studying for her finals, not in a Mexican jail."

While Myrtle was speaking, the door opened and Mac walked in. He smiled when he saw me, and I smiled back. I hadn't seen him since Sunday when he'd helped me move to the Livingstons', after which he'd taken over my apartment. Since then he'd had late shifts, so it was lovely to see him unexpectedly. But then, seeing him was always lovely.

"Ah, Mac. Just in time," Josephine said. She introduced him to Philippa and to Norman Neumann, who up to now had sat off to the side, watching the proceedings without speaking.

"Okay," Lillian said. "Our next skit will be Mac trying to convince Norman that he's missed responding to a jury summons, and if he doesn't pay a fine right away, he'll be held in contempt of court and jailed."

Myrtle and I gave up our places at the table to the men. As Mac and I passed each other, he touched my hand.

While I'd thought of several ways Myrtle could have verified whether her caller was indeed her granddaughter, the second skit presented a more complex situation. I knew if I got such a call, I'd simply ask Mac for advice, but I thought at least some people would pay the fine as quickly as possible. Especially if the caller was as convincing as Mac was with the help of Philippa's script. Then it occurred to me. The scammers probably also had scripts.

Norman was great, playing the nervous member of the public now caught up in a legal mess. After intimidating him, Mac gave him a number to call to pay his fine. At that point, Lillian stepped in to say the audience would again be asked for suggestions of how to determine if the call was legitimate.

Mac and Philippa then did two mini scenes, with Mac first playing a bogus IRS employee calling to tell Philippa she owed back taxes and would be taken before a grand jury if she didn't make immediate arrangements to pay. The second was Mac as a fake Social Security Administration employee trying to get Philippa to give him her personal information.

The final skit had me calling Lillian to tell her she had won a ten-thousand-dollar sweepstakes. All she had to do was pay a small administrative fee and give me her bank account number so the money could be deposited. Lillian played the initially ecstatic but increasingly skeptical "winner" to the hilt, and we ended up laughing together.

Partway through the scene with Lillian, Mac left, waving to me on his way out.

When we finished, we gathered around the table to critique the skits. After that, Josephine invited me to stay for dinner. Since Mac was working late again, I accepted.

"So that's Norman," I said as Josephine poured us tea. "You're right," I told Lillian. "He's quite distinguished looking. And you're also right that Myrtle has her eye on him."

"I think Norman prefers Josephine, but she won't listen."

"You've all been pushing Norman on me so hard, I had him investigated," Josephine said, not batting an eye at Lillian's assertion that Norman liked her.

"Did you. And did you find out anything interesting?" Lillian said.

"I did indeed. For one thing, the man isn't who he says he is."

"Really? Then who is he?"

"His name is Norman Neumann, all right. But he was no more a forensic accountant than I was a ballerina."

"What was he then?"

"Still is. A partner in the firm Neumann & Purcell." Josephine sat back with a satisfied smirk.

"He's a lawyer?" Lillian said.

"Not exactly."

"Okay, Josephine, you've toyed with us enough." Lillian sounded stern. "Out with it, girl."

"Neumann & Purcell specializes in the recovery of stolen art and antiquities."

"Then why on earth would he tell you he was an accountant?" Lillian said. "And what's he doing working here as an activities director?"

"I can think of one reason," I said. Their heads turned and they stared at me. "He's on a case."

Josephine sat back, blinking. "You know, he did ask me about my painting, ten seconds after we met."

"Is there any doubt of the painting's provenance?" I asked.

"Absolutely none. I bought it from a reputable gallery. And before approaching the museum, I had my lawyer double-check."

"It's still odd that someone who specializes in recovering lost art would show up here so soon after your son discovered the painting on your wall," I said.

Josephine, looking distracted, took a sip of tea.

"Well," Lillian said, "it was getting awfully dull around here. This might spice things up considerably."

"Your lives may be dull, but Mac's ex-wife is enough spice for me."

"Has something else happened?" Josephine asked.

"She just told Mac this weekend she's expecting twins."

"Oh dear. That can't be good."

"I suppose it depends on your point of view. She came to see me, you know."

"Uh-oh."

"Uh-oh indeed. It was like being caught in the middle of a soap opera. She's pretending she and Mac are still married."

"We know that's not true," Josephine said.

"It doesn't make him any less trapped. You see, he can't bring himself to kick her out. But the good news is I got a house-sitting gig for the next year. Great big place near the safety center. I moved into the mother-in-law suite last weekend, and Mac moved into my apartment to get away from Lisa."

"How'd she respond to that?" Lillian asked.

"I don't think he's told her yet. He waited until she left for work to move his stuff, and he's been working late shifts this past week. I doubt she'll be happy, though. She told him she made a mistake divorcing him."

"What does he say about that?"

"You do know Mac doesn't talk much about how he's feeling. But I know he finds it all deeply disturbing. We both do."

"You know, if we were talking about any man besides Mac, I'd suggest both DNA testing and a thorough background check on the two of them." Josephine frowned.

"But although Mac's just proved he's a good actor, I don't believe he can hide his essential character."

"I understand him not being able to toss her out while she's pregnant. What I worry about is what happens when the babies arrive. I think that'll make everything even more complicated. And at the moment, neither of us sees a way out."

"I'm sure there is one." Josephine looked thoughtful. "I'll bet she can be bought off."

"Yes, I'm sure she can, but Mac and I need to solve our own problems, so please promise me you won't interfere."

Josephine sighed. "And you know I have more money than I can ever get through, even if I go on a yacht-buying spree. So if money will solve it, all you have to do is ask."

"It's tempting. Really, it is. And thank you for the offer, but no. I don't think it's a good idea."

"I agree with Devi," Lillian said. "Difficulties like this aren't meant to be overcome easily."

Chapter Twenty-Two

Josephine

After discovering who Norman Neumann really was, I suspected my son, Jeff, had hired him to locate the painting. In the last couple of weeks, Jeff's phone calls, full of whining and wheedling and insisting he needed to talk to me, had ramped up. Although I could continue to ignore my son, I decided to confront Norman.

He made that easy by coming up to me after breakfast and suggesting a meeting to talk about the workshop handout. I swallowed my apprehension about being alone with him and invited him to my apartment. After all, there are handy emergency pull cords in every room.

After he was seated at the table where a draft copy of the handout was awaiting him, I asked if he'd like a cup of tea. That showed how nervous I was, since it had been my intention to get this interaction over with as quickly as possible.

"Sorry. I'm not much of a tea drinker. But I wouldn't say no to coffee if you have it made."

"I don't, but it takes only a minute."

Not liking tea was yet another strike to add to the several he'd already accumulated. I went to the kitchen and set the coffeemaker to one cup.

Then I sat across from him. He'd been reading the handout, but when I sat down, he looked up with a grin and gestured toward my living room.

"I like what you've done with the place, Jo."

Jo? "That was quite a leap you just took, Mr. Neumann."

"Leap?"

"From Mrs. Bartlett all the way to Jo."

"Without spending time calling you Josephine, you mean." He shrugged. "The formality was getting to be too much. Besides, you look more like a Jo to me than a Josephine."

There'd been only one person in my life who called me Jo. Daniel. The only man I ever loved. Devi knew that story, but I'd not told anyone else.

I took a sip of tea and examined Norman. His current expression was clearly the one that had etched the fan of smile lines into the corners of his eyes.

"And I really do like what you've done with the place."

"I lived with mahogany monstrosities and gilt frames far too long."

"If this is your taste, that had to be difficult."

It had been difficult, but in ways I was unwilling to share with Norman. The coffeemaker finished burbling, and I got up to pour his cup. "Milk or sugar?"

He shook his head. "Black. Thanks." He took the cup, sipped, and smiled. "Excellent. An Ethiopian dark, perhaps?"

Although I drink coffee only occasionally, when I do, I want something that matches my teas in quality.

"You're full of surprises." His expression was thoughtful.

"As are you. What I want to know is are you enjoying your retirement? Is it everything you dreamed it would be?"

"I believe you're teasing me. I am still working, you know. Even if it is a temporary position." He took another appreciative sip of coffee, before looking at me over the rim of the cup.

"Indeed. About that. Doesn't your partner...Mr. Purcell, miss you?"

Grinning, he set the cup down and rested his chin on his hands. "Why, Jo, I do believe you've been investigating me."

"I've found it to be an excellent strategy when I suspect someone is investigating me."

He sat for a moment, staring at me; then he picked up his cup and took another sip. I waited for what would come next.

"Is there a reason I should investigate you?" he asked.

"Not that I know of. And yet it seems you are." Although he was admitting nothing, I was convinced my guess was right and that my Hopper painting had to be the focus of his interest. "Did my son hire you?"

He blinked, looking surprised. "Your son?"

It was unclear whether his surprise was because my guess was correct, or because he had no connection to Jeff.

"Jeff Bartlett?"

He shook his head. "No."

"But you are investigating me."

He didn't answer, an answer of sorts.

A thought about what to do next popped into my head. Without debating it, I decided to go for it. After all, seeing is believing, and if I wanted to convince Norman to give up whatever quest he was on, either at Jeff's behest or on his own behalf, the best approach was to show him the painting.

"You don't happen to have a couple of hours free, do you?"

He shrugged. "There's nothing on the schedule until this afternoon."

"Tell you what. Get your coat and meet me by the back door in five minutes."

"We're going somewhere?"

"We are."

After I closed the door on Norman, I called Lill to see if she would come along, but she said absolutely not. Sighing in resignation and beginning to regret my plan before it even got off the ground, I made a second call to Devi, then put on my coat and grabbed my purse and car keys.

I found Norman standing outside in the cold by the back door. I gestured toward my car, a neon-green Subaru Crosstrek Devi helped me pick out.

"Great color," Norman said, opening the driver's door for me.

"That's the main reason I picked it, but I'm also partial to the way it handles."

He climbed into the passenger seat and snapped his seat belt. "Are we going far?"

"You could just wait and see." I started the car and pulled out of my parking spot.

"Nice weather we're having," he said.

I glanced at him to see those smile lines were once again engaged.

"How about those Bengals?" I replied.

"You do realize football season ended some time ago?"

"Did it?"

"It did. It's almost time for spring training."

"How about those Reds?" I turned onto the street leading to an on-ramp to the interstate.

"Are there any sports you do follow?" he asked.

"I'm rather taken with that golfer. Jordan Spieth."

"Because you like golf?"

"Not especially. What about you? Are you really a Bengals fan?" If he was, I was prepared to downgrade considerably my impression of his intelligence.

"It's a useful topic of conversation. But the truth is I'd rather read a good book, or even a not-so-good book, than watch a game."

By this point, we'd made it to the highway. I glanced at him to find he had a thoughtful look.

"You know," he said, "you're not at all what I expected."

"Why were you expecting anything?"

"Candace gave me a rundown on the more prominent residents when I first came. You made the list."

I avoided responding by concentrating on changing lanes.

"Aren't you curious what she told me?"

"I think I can guess."

"She said, and I'm quoting here, 'Josephine Bartlett will chew you up and spit you out without a second thought.'"

It stung, but I knew Candace was probably referring to my role in getting Mr. Souter, the previous manager, fired. She'd had a cozy berth with Souter in charge. Not so cozy since the new manager took over.

"She's out of date. I've given up human flesh."

"Good to know," Norman said. "Makes being trapped with you in this small space much less threatening."

"I also make it a rule never to eat while I'm driving."

That made Norman chuckle, and I couldn't help smiling as well. Which wasn't the way I'd expected this interaction to go.

After twenty minutes, I exited the interstate, and when I turned to drive up the hill into Eden Park, Norman chuckled again. "Let me guess. We're going to the art museum."

Without responding, I lowered my window and gave the parking attendant my name, and he said he'd let Ms. Subramanian know I'd arrived.

Once I'd parked, Norman and I walked in the museum's front entrance, a formal Grecian affair with huge columns and tall windows. As we crossed the lobby, Devi came to greet us. She gave me a quick hug, something she's taken to doing since the shooting. Then she greeted Norman.

"So nice to see you again, Mr. Neumann."

"Please. Call me Norman."

"Okay. Norman it is. If you'd both follow me..."

Norman gave me a look but said nothing as Devi led us to the stairs to the basement.

When we reached the section where the Hopper was currently stored, Devi stepped up to the painting and lifted the protective cover while I watched Norman's reaction. His expression registered surprise followed by comprehension. Clearly, he was a person who could move from A to Z with little explanation.

"I take it this is your painting?" Although he didn't take his eyes off *Sea Watchers,* he directed the words at me.

"It is. And its provenance is impeccable."

"And it's here because...?"

"After my son outed me, I couldn't keep it at Brookside, so I arranged for it to come here on a long-term loan."

"We'll be hanging it in one of the public galleries soon," Devi said. "We just have to arrange appropriate fanfare to greet its arrival."

"Well, Jo, it looks very much like I owe you an apology."

Devi looked at me, her hand to her mouth, obviously to stifle a snort of amusement.

I rolled my eyes at her. "Norman here insists I look more like a Jo than a Josephine, and short of threatening him with bodily harm, I don't know how to stop him."

Devi laughed. "I love it. Jo. Can I call you Jo?"

"If Norman is going to insist on doing it—"

"And I am," he said. Then he looked at his watch. "It's almost noon. How about I take you two ladies to lunch?"

Devi looked at her own watch. "Sorry, I can't come. Meeting in a few. You two are on your own."

I gave her a look. She shrugged, a bland expression on her face. No question, she was lying about the meeting. But then, I had shoved her into Mac's arms. I could hardly complain if she did a little shoving of her own.

She led us back upstairs.

"Do you want to see where the painting will hang?" I asked Norman.

"I assume in the gallery with the other Hopper painting."

"Yes."

"Then I'll just wait until the big day."

We reached the corridor that led to the museum's restaurant. "I know we could have lunch here," he said. "But I have another suggestion."

"What's that?"

"You could just wait and see."

"But since I'll be driving..."

"I'll direct you."

We walked back to the car, and with Norman telling me where to turn, we soon arrived at the Banks area along the Ohio River. I parked in the garage across from the baseball stadium, and Norman led the way into a restaurant that had huge windows overlooking the river and northern Kentucky.

After we ordered, Norman handed his menu to the server and then, his expression serious, he looked at me. "If you don't want me to, I won't call you Jo."

"I thought you intended to insist upon it."

"Not if you object. Do you object?"

"I...it feels odd. It's been a long time since someone called me Jo."

"If you decide you don't like it, let me know."

The waiter showed up with a basket of bread, an interruption I very much welcomed as it gave me a moment to compose what I next wanted to say to him.

"You haven't yet told me why you were investigating me."

"What gave me away?"

"You don't deny it?"

He shook his head.

"For one thing, being an activities director seemed like an odd second career choice for a forensic accountant."

"Associate activities director."

"Even more suspicious. Anyway, it made me curious enough to check on you. But what I want to know is—what's your interest in me?"

"Maybe I'd better start at the beginning. As you discovered, I'm in the business of recovering stolen art." He glanced at me, and I nodded. "And for the past forty years, one particular case has stymied me and my partner. Are you familiar with the Elizabeth Kent Oakes Museum heist?"

"Yes, of course. I was living in Boston when it happened. Oh," I said, doing a quick jump from A to Z of my own. "You thought I had something to do with that?"

"A Hopper was included in the haul. And when I asked you an innocuous question about your painting, you did a very nice job of deflecting me. Then I discovered you'd been living in Boston at the time of the robbery, and that raised my level of suspicion even higher. But my investigation stalled when I couldn't find anyone who'd seen your painting and could describe it for me."

"Lill could have."

"But she didn't. She was just as vague as you were. So you see, I had to get to know you better, hoping you'd eventually tell me about the painting, or maybe I'd discover additional evidence linking you to the EKO heist."

I sat back, and instead of examining him, I looked out the window at a tug shoving a long line of barges downriver. "You know, I'd forgotten there was a Hopper painting taken in that robbery."

"Actually, it was an odd choice, since at the time it was worth only thousands of dollars, while the other works taken were worth millions. It was also the only modern work included. My partner and I have always suspected one of the thieves simply liked it. So when I heard about your Hopper—"

"You thought I was one of the thieves."

"Or your husband was."

"Besides me, what other suspects do you have?"

He shook his head, his lips thinning. "Not a one."

"What do you know about the thieves?"

"Very little, I'm afraid. The museum didn't have video cameras, and the guards were taken by surprise and didn't see faces. One guard claimed he saw the shadows of three people right before someone tackled him from behind and handcuffed and blindfolded him. He was a big guy, so we assume the tackler was a man. But the other two thieves could have been women. And given forty years has passed, all the thieves will be, at the very least, in their sixties."

"Hence the retirement community connection."

"It did make the information worth checking."

"But how did you hear about my painting?"

"One of my partner's former neighbors lives at Brookside. Bertie Teller? Perhaps you know him."

"Of course. Myrtle's innamorato."

"Her what?"

"Since you arrived, Myrtle's been pretending she's available. But before that, she and Bertie were involved in the romance of the century."

Norman sat back, shaking his head and grinning. "How about you, Jo? Any admirers?"

"Nary a one."

He gave me an odd look that I was able to ignore when the waiter showed up with perfect timing to deliver our lunch plates.

I waited until he'd served us and moved away. "Forty years is a long time without a hint who the thieves are."

"That's why we followed this lead so aggressively. Our biggest fear is that the thieves will die before we find out who they are, and with that goes our best chance of recovering the paintings. But now we're back at square one." He sighed.

"Are you certain I'm not your thief? After all, just because I have a legitimate Hopper doesn't mean I don't have an ill-gotten one stashed under my bed."

His eyebrows went up. "Do you?"

I shook my head. "I suppose this means you'll be leaving Brookside?" The thought brought with it a discomfort I didn't wish to explore further.

He shrugged. "I probably need to give at least a two-week notice, don't you think?"

"I'm sure Candace would appreciate it."

When Norman gestured to the waiter to bring the check, I didn't even open my mouth to offer to pay my share. I thought he owed me more than a lunch for ever having suspected me.

Chapter Twenty-Three

Devi

I drove straight from work to Josephine's, worrying the whole way she'd be annoyed with me for skipping out on lunch in such an obvious way. But when I knocked on her door, she answered promptly and invited me in with a smile.

"How was your lunch?" I asked.

"How was your meeting?" she responded.

"Excellent."

"So was my lunch."

"Are you going to tell me what you discovered? Is Norman investigating you?"

"He was. He now claims he sees the error of his ways."

"Why was he investigating you?"

"You're familiar with the Elizabeth Kent Oaks heist?"

"Of course. It's a major case study for museums of what not to do security-wise. Wait, he thought you had something to do with that?"

"After he heard about my Hopper painting, he discovered I was living in Boston when the robbery took place. And he put two and two together."

"He told you all that?"

"He did."

"And you said?"

"By that time he'd seen the painting and knew it wasn't the one that was stolen."

"So, once the two of you got that cleared up, did you enjoy your...date?" And trust me, I knew the chance I was taking using the word "date." But I thought it was worth it.

Josephine blushed. A first. "It wasn't a date. We had a nice lunch and a mutually enlightening conversation, and that was it."

"Oh," I said. "It just occurred to me. If he's no longer investigating you, he'll be leaving Brookside."

"Yes. He will. So everyone can climb off the fixing-up-Josephine train and get on with their lives."

"Where does he live?"

She cleared her throat. "Indian Hill."

Even I knew that was Cincinnati's most expensive and exclusive suburb. Josephine held up a hand to ward off my squeal of delight.

"But he likes you."

"And you know that because?"

"During the rehearsal the other day, I watched him, and he was paying more attention to you than to anything or anyone else."

"Because he suspected me of being the mastermind behind the EKO robbery."

"If you say so."

"I do."

"So how does it feel to be on the being-fixed-up receiving end for a change," I teased her.

"You didn't like it and neither do I. And isn't it time for you to go fix Mac's dinner or something?"

We gave each other looks, but because I didn't have Josephine's experience looking stern, I quickly dissolved into giggles. After a moment, she chuckled, something I doubt she would have done four months ago.

Chapter Twenty-Four

Mac

When I talked to the chief about the scams-and-cons workshop, he not only gave me permission to spend work time on it, he said he'd be attending the inaugural performance. So shortly before three on Wednesday, the two of us met at Brookside.

I introduced him to Norman, Lillian, Philippa, and Josephine, then we took seats in the back of the room. About that time, Devi arrived, and I watched as a ripple of awareness flowed through the crowd. In the next moment, residents with and without walkers and canes surrounded her, all of them reaching out to touch her, or if they were positioned close enough, to hug her.

I had a sudden unwelcome image of Lisa walking into a room like this under similar circumstances and knew the reaction to her would not have been nearly as warm. For the first time, I let myself consider the possibility I'd married Lisa more because of her outer than her inner beauty.

Devi had both. I took a deep breath and let it out slowly, relaxing into the knowledge of how much I loved her.

"When do you go on?" the chief asked as the crowd settled.

"I'm in the second and third scenes," I told him.

"Nervous?"

I grinned at him. "I don't think anyone will throw rotten tomatoes if I mess up a line, if that's what you mean."

"That's the young woman who was shot, isn't it?" He gestured with his chin toward Devi, who had taken her place at the front of the room with Myrtle. The contrast between the two women was startling, and not only because Myrtle had fifty years and two hundred pounds on Devi.

"Yes, it is." *And I want her to marry me.*

Maybe if I practiced the words, even silently, I might find it possible to say them out loud to Devi sometime soon. Meanwhile, they took up residence in my head, like an annoying jingle that couldn't be dislodged. Although this was one song I wanted to hold on to.

As I adjusted to the idea, Josephine moved to the front of the room and spoke briefly about the purpose of the workshop. Then she introduced Devi, to loud clapping and shouts of approval, and Myrtle, who inclined her head in response to the continued clapping, channeling Queen Elizabeth, if I wasn't mistaken.

A phone rang, and Devi and Myrtle launched into the grandchild-in-trouble skit, which I'd missed seeing during our rehearsal. Devi did a great job of sounding distressed. So good, it made my gut tighten until I reminded myself she was acting.

As the scene progressed, I heard a gasp. I tried to pin down where it came from, but it was unclear. Then Josephine stepped in to ask the audience to suggest how Myrtle could have unmasked the caller, and a hand went up with its owner admitting she'd already fallen for the scam.

"I didn't know what to do when I found out," the woman said. "It was dreadfully upsetting. And embarrassing."

And frustrating. There's so little we can do to help victims. The criminals are rarely in our jurisdiction and, even if they are, the methods they use are usually impossible for a local department with limited resources to trace.

"How did you discover it was a scam?" Josephine asked the woman.

"My grandson called me a couple of days later, and when I asked him how everything worked out, he didn't know what

I was talking about. I bought a thousand dollars' worth of those green cards they told you to use, Myrtle." The woman's voice quavered.

Looking at Josephine, I could tell she was furious that the woman had been taken advantage of.

"I fell for it as well." A man this time. "But make that a granddaughter and two thousand dollars. And the person who called to tell me my granddaughter was in trouble said he was from the police."

That started a spirited discussion about what to do if any of them got such a call in the future. The chief had the unpleasant task of telling them once they gave the criminals the numbers on the money-transfer cards, the money was unrecoverable.

"The best defense is always to be suspicious of any requests for money or personal information even from someone claiming to be a policeman. That's the only way to stop these folks from getting their hands on what belongs to you," he said.

After fifteen minutes, Josephine cut off the discussion so Norman and I could take our places.

After the first skit with Norman about missing jury duty, Josephine introduced the second set of skits where I tried to con Philippa, first into thinking she owed the IRS money and then into thinking I was a Social Security employee who had a legitimate need for her to provide me with her personal data.

"Oh yes, I've gotten that IRS call," said a woman in the front row. "And the social security call," said another.

*So have I*s and *me too*s echoed around the room.

Josephine asked how they'd responded to the calls, and then she asked the chief for more suggestions of what to do. The main strategy, the chief reminded them, was to remember that the IRS and Social Security Administration never called taxpayers. "Best approach to a call like that is to hang up."

"After telling them to go stuff themselves!" said one of the few men in the room.

"What about the jury-duty call?" Josephine said. "Nobody's gotten that one?"

A man raised his hand, looking sheepish. "And you're right. I couldn't wait to pay the fine and get all square."

"So if it happened again, you'd...?" Josephine said.

"Why, I'd call the detective here. He'd know what to do." The man nodded toward me.

"We'd be happy to check with the court for you," I assured the man.

The final skit was Devi and Lillian doing a you've-won-a-sweepstakes scam.

"You might also get this one in the mail," Josephine said in summary.

Again, several people pitched in to say they'd gotten either a phone call or a mailing informing them they'd won big, and they needed only to pay a small fee or provide their bank account number to collect their prize. While nobody admitted to having fallen for it, I saw heads nodding in recognition of the ploy.

"Bottom line," Josephine said, wrapping up the ensuing discussion, "if it sounds too good to be true, it probably is."

"Or too bad to be true," the woman who'd fallen for the grandchild scam said to laughter.

"Always talk to someone who can assist you if anyone asks you for money or bank information. Even requests from people claiming to be members of your family should be double-checked. Mrs. Gowan, our manager, can help as can Detective McElroy or anyone else in his department. I urge you, don't ever transfer money or provide personal information unless you're sure it's for a legitimate purpose."

After another round of applause, the room gradually began to empty.

"Excellent," the chief said. "Even though we can't do much once they send money, spreading the word to prevent it before it happens is a good approach. And anything you can do to help with this effort, you have my approval."

"Josephine and Lillian have talked about visiting other retirement communities."

"Great idea. If they need you, just report the times you'll be involved. That is, if you want to be?"

"I do."

"Good. Good work, Detective."

He left, and I stood waiting for Devi. She finished speaking with the last resident and then she walked up to me, smiling. My lips stretched wide in a matching grin.

"Missed you," she said.

"I know. Bad schedule this past week. Dinner tonight?"

"Lovely. My place or yours?"

"They're both yours. But I guess I'd prefer it if you came to the apartment. If you don't mind?"

"Thank goodness the Livingstons leave soon."

Josephine joined us at that point, and I told her what the chief had said about the workshop and my involvement.

"It went well, don't you think? We may have to replace Norman, but it's good to know you can join us, Mac."

"Why do you have to replace Norman?" I asked.

"Because shortly he'll be returning to his regularly scheduled life."

"Which is?"

"It's a long story. Devi knows part of it. Why don't you both come to dinner Saturday, and I'll tell you all about it."

I glanced at Devi, who nodded.

"Done," I said.

~ ~ ~

After the workshop, I still had some things to finish up at the office, but as soon as I'd finished, I drove to Devi's apartment where I was now living. I opened the door to the smell of dinner cooking and Devi standing there, waiting to step into my arms.

I nuzzled her neck. "I could get used to this." And what was I waiting for to be more definitive? Some stupid timetable imposed by my ex-wife? "I love you, Devi."

"And I love you, Mac. I have for quite a while, you know."

"Me too. Don't know why it took me so long to tell you."

Lisa had expected me to make a big deal of the proposal. I hoped all Devi would need was heartfelt sincerity. "Marry me?"

She pulled back and grinned at me. "Just try to get out of it, Detective." She snuggled against me, and I stood there holding her, reveling in such pure happiness, I was halfway convinced I was dreaming.

"Come." She took my hand and led me to the kitchen where she took a seat kitty-corner from me. Her knees were touching mine and she was still holding my hand. With the other hand, she cupped my cheek. "Do you have any idea how much I love you?"

"I'm getting a pretty good idea." We grinned at each other like kids plotting an elaborate prank. "How soon do you think we can manage a wedding?" Now that I'd declared myself, I couldn't wait to take the next step.

"I want my parents to come. So, June?"

"You don't want to get married in Kansas?"

She shook her head. "This is my home now. You're my home."

Something sputtered on the stove, and Devi jumped to her feet to pull the pot off the burner. That broke the spell and reminded me to slow down. Devi looked great, but only a few weeks ago she'd nearly died.

That thought, that I'd come so close to losing her, made my mouth dry out. To counter that, along with my desire for more than hugs and kisses, I went and opened the box of Erdradour Scotch.

When I brought the bottle to the kitchen, Devi smiled. "I wondered when you were going to open a bottle of that."

"You realize if I sold it off, it would take care of most of my debt?" I pulled a glass from the cupboard and poured a small dram.

"Now that's a thought. Can you do that?"

"Probably not the best idea. Would you like some?"

"Actually, I've never tasted Scotch." She cocked her head in obvious query.

"Here, take a small sip. Hold it in your mouth to warm it and then let it slide down your throat."

She took the glass from my hand and sipped. She looked at me, her eyes widening. Then she swallowed. "Umm. That was—"

Before she could say more, I kissed her, tasting her freshness overlaid with smoke.

"Oh." She breathed against my lips. "That was...lovely."

If we didn't stop, it would take little more to make stopping very difficult. I stepped away from her, laying my hand on her head. "You know, if you keep doing things like that, you need to be aware there are consequences."

"You know what I want, Mac? Right now."

I cleared my throat. "Another sip of Scotch?"

She shook her head, then took me by the hand and led me to the bedroom. Luckily, I'd pulled the covers up that morning and picked up most of my dirty clothes.

"I thought no sex for another couple of weeks." My voice was husky and I was having difficulty remembering to breathe.

She began unbuttoning my shirt. "There are other things we can do."

She pushed my shirt out of the way and then pulled off her own shirt. In a remarkably short time, we were naked and lying spooned together under the quilt.

"Did you know babies need to be cuddled or they don't thrive?" she said.

"Can't say I knew that."

She'd slipped into bed so quickly, I'd not had a chance to look at her, so now I let my fingers explore the smooth silk of her skin until I encountered the unevenness of the scar on her side. I touched it lightly. "Does this hurt?"

"No. Not now. Sometimes it itches or burns. But if you keep touching it that way, soon it won't hurt at all."

"What took us so long," I said, breathing against her neck.

She shivered in response. "Just stubborn, I guess. But then the best things are worth the wait."

Amen to that.

Chapter Twenty-Five

Josephine

The phone rang. I checked caller ID the way I always do to be sure to avoid calls from Jeff. Since this call was from the Brookside front office, I answered.

"Jo, it's Norman."

"Yes?"

"I'm calling to ask you to dinner this evening."

"You want me to save you a place?"

"No. I'll come and pick you up, and we'll drive to a restaurant and have dinner. Just the two of us."

"Why do you want to do that?"

"Hmm. Well, for one thing, I'm still feeling guilty about suspecting you."

"What's the other?"

"What?"

"The other thing? You said guilt is only one of the reasons."

"The other is..." He cleared his throat. "I enjoyed our lunch and I hate eating alone."

"That's two."

"It is, isn't it."

"Which just goes to show, you were right not to choose forensic accounting as a career."

"So, will you go to dinner with me?"

"Yes. Okay. What time?"

"Six all right with you?"

Although it was already four, I told him it was okay and hung up, frowning. What an extremely peculiar invitation.

Still puzzling over it, I called Lill to tell her I wouldn't be at dinner this evening.

"You're not ill, are you?"

"No. I'm fine. I just...the truth is, Norman called and invited me to have dinner out."

"And you said yes? Way to go, Josephine."

"You don't need to sound so gleeful. It's only dinner."

"It's a date. I bet you haven't had one of those in fifty years. And you do know people kiss on first dates these days? Or so I've been told."

"They also have sex, if you believe what you read. Doesn't mean I have to."

"Of course not. But don't rule it out before you try it."

"See? That's exactly the reason I didn't want to tell you."

I hung up on the sound of Lill chortling, and went to examine my closet for something to wear that was a notch above casual but not dressy enough to give Norman any more ideas than he already seemed to have.

~ ~ ~

When we arrived at the restaurant, Norman helped me with my coat before sliding into the booth across from me. He cocked his head and smiled. "You look beautiful tonight, Jo."

He didn't look bad himself in a sports coat over a collared shirt but without a tie, striking the same semi-casual note I'd aimed for.

We were handed menus when we were seated, and now the waiter arrived to ask if we'd like to order drinks. After a quick consult, Norman ordered us both glasses of pinot grigio.

"So, did you ask me out to tell me I'm back on your suspect list?"

"I asked you out because it's been a long time since I enjoyed talking to someone as much as I've enjoyed my conversations with you."

"All three of them?"

"I believe it's more like four or possibly five. But the fact you're counting gives me hope."

"Of what?"

"That you might one day admit me to your circle of friends."

The waiter chose that moment to deliver our wine, so I let the comment go by without an answer. But as I sat across from Norman in the subdued light, watching as he looked up at the waiter and smiled, the past rushed in.

For a moment, the impression I was sitting across from Daniel was so strong I could almost smell his aftershave. But then the scene altered, and I realized I could no longer focus because my eyes had filled with tears. I lowered my head and got out a tissue to blow my nose, blinking away the wetness, hoping Norman hadn't noticed.

Perhaps he hadn't because when I looked up he was still interacting with the waiter, who had apparently recited the specials while I was lost in the past. I bowed my head again, trying to make sense of the menu as the waiter took his leave and Norman raised his glass.

"To friendship," he said.

I raised my own glass and tapped it lightly against his. Took a sip.

"Do you know what you want?" he asked.

Daniel. I wanted Daniel. Or what I had with Daniel. But finding that again at this late date was about as likely as me levitating and swooping around the restaurant, sprinkling fairy dust on everyone. I shook my head to clear it.

"The special sounded good," he said.

"Which one?" Luckily there's always more than one.

We spent the next several minutes negotiating what to order while I tried to banish the past.

"My wife and I used to eat out a lot," he said after we'd finished ordering. "I miss having someone to share with." He'd suggested we share an appetizer and a salad.

"My husband never shared."

"That's too bad."

"Yes. It was." He'd also neither loved nor respected me.

We seemed to have marooned ourselves on some impossible conversational shoal. I took a sip of wine, wishing the waiter would drop by with a question, a salad, a tiny taste offering from the chef, something.

"You don't want to talk about him."

"No. I don't."

"The heavy mahogany and gilt frames?"

"Yes."

"I suppose it is tacky to bring up the past when you're hoping to build something new. But before we leave the past completely, I'd love to know more about the painting."

"What do you want to know?"

"How you happened to buy it? And where?"

"Still suspicious?"

"Not at all. Just curious."

"I bought it on a trip to New York. By chance, I walked into the gallery where it was for sale." *And met Daniel.* "I'd recently had a stock split, and I decided to cash in my profits and splurge."

Our salads arrived, and I was able to stop the story there. While we ate, Norman asked me to fill in the information he'd heard about the recent goings-on at Brookside. Since most of it was public knowledge, I obliged.

"You're fond of Devi, aren't you," he said when I finished.

"I am. She's very dear to me."

"What about children? Do you have any?"

"I have a son." I closed my lips over the rim of my wineglass.

"Hmm. Something else you don't want to talk about."

"Yes. And you? Any children?"

His fork stopped in midair and his expression turned anguished. "A daughter who lives in Colorado. And a son...who was killed in Iraq."

117

"I'm so sorry." I looked down at my plate to give him a moment to recover.

"It's impossible to get to our age without losses," he said after a bit.

"Yes."

"You don't have to tiptoe around it on my account, though. Yes, I miss my wife and my son. I always will, but I don't want to feel that I can never mention them again."

"You're right. If we avoid all the painful aspects of our lives, we'll likely have little to talk about."

But despite our brave words, we were both silent for a time after that. I didn't know what he was thinking, but I was thinking how ironic life so often seems to be, with the latest example being him losing a son he clearly loved while I was estranged from my still-very-much-alive son who was also my least favorite person on the planet.

Eventually, we began talking about less personal topics. At the end of the meal, he suggested we share a dessert and then he drove me back to Brookside. He walked me to my door and leaned in to kiss me on the cheek.

"I hope you'll be willing to do this again soon, Jo."

I'd turned to unlock my door, but now I turned back and looked at him. At a man who appeared fit and was trim, without the midriff bulge most men of his age sported. At a face that was no longer young, but carried its years well. I've heard it said we end up with the face we deserve. If that's true, Norman's been a good person.

"Do you like Scotch?" The words rushed out before I could corral them.

He blinked and cocked his head. "Is that a requirement?"

"Well?"

"As a matter of fact, I do. Very much."

"How about a nightcap then?"

When he nodded, I opened the door and he followed me inside. I pulled the bottle of Erdradour out of the credenza along with a glass, poured two fingers, and handed it to him.

"Wait, you're not joining me?"

"I prefer tea. And Mac tells me it's a shame to waste even a drop of that on anyone who doesn't appreciate what they're drinking."

Norman took a slow sip and then smiled. "He's right. This is exceptional." He picked up the bottle and read the label, then took another sip, closing his eyes as he did so.

He swirled the liquid in his glass. "I owe you another couple of dinners for this."

Then he smiled at me, and I was quite glad of that debt.

Chapter Twenty-Six

Mac

In the week after I'd moved into Devi's apartment after she moved to the Livingstons', Lisa called my cell several times from either her school phone or my house. Whenever I saw either number on caller ID, I let the call go to voice mail.

Her messages were short but increasingly agitated—all saying the same thing. That she needed to speak to me.

I knew the conversation wouldn't please either of us, so I continued trying to avoid it, although I knew I'd have to contact her eventually.

She beat me to it by showing up at Devi's place Saturday morning. When I answered the door, she nodded as if unsurprised to see me there, then pushed past me into the apartment.

"We need to talk, Darren." As she spoke, she did a quick check of the bedroom and bathroom, then turned to me with a puzzled expression.

It was clear what she was thinking—where was Devi? I decided to force her to say it. Instead, she nodded to herself, took a seat at one end of the couch, and patted the cushion beside her. Ignoring her obvious command, I pulled a chair from its position at the table and sat facing her across the coffee table. Leaning back, I waited for her to begin.

"I see you've moved out of the house. Is that permanent?"

"Yes."

"What about the rent?"

"You mean who pays it?"

She nodded.

"Since you haven't lost your job or your insurance, I think you should. It's due by the fifth of the month."

"That's cold, Darren."

"Not as cold as you moving in and expecting me to pay for everything. Not to mention telling everyone we remarried."

"Oh. Did I upset the girlfriend cart for you?"

I folded my arms and waited.

She shrugged. "Sorry about that."

"No. I don't believe you are. You said we needed to talk. So talk."

"I just...need to know your plans?"

"Why?"

She swallowed. "I'm not safe yet. They could terminate me at the end of the school year, and there would go my insurance."

"You teach science. You should have no difficulty finding another position." I was tired of her holding the possible loss of medical insurance over my head. The fact she was pregnant had been evident for weeks. If the school was going to fire her for that, they should have done it already.

"Right. Sure. Everyone is just dying to hire the single mother of twins."

"Lots of single mothers work."

"You don't care what happens to me, do you?"

"If I didn't care, I would have changed the locks one day when you were at school."

"But that might harm your image as Saint Darren, the big-hearted."

"What did you want to talk about," I gave in and rubbed my head, which was beginning to ache.

"Child support."

"Why do we need to talk about that?"

"I lied. About the affair. The babies are yours. And mine."

"What?" I'd been sitting back, but now I leaned forward and the chair thumped down. "That's not possible. And you know it."

"Of course it's possible."

"No. It's not."

"Oh, Darren. O ye of little faith." She sat there, shaking her head at me as if I were one of her students who had just said something incredibly stupid.

And then it dawned on me. There was one way what she was saying might be physically possible. But that same way would have been financially impossible. Or so I thought.

"I had a lottery win last March," Lisa said, an amused look on her face. "One of the smaller prizes, but enough for one last try. If you recall, we didn't use all the embryos."

"Why didn't you tell me? Why make up a story?"

She looked away, her shoulders beginning to shake. "I thought I could make you love me again."

"How do I know you're telling the truth this time?" Even more important, I didn't want to believe anything she'd said.

"I thought you might not believe me." She sniffled and pulled a couple of documents out of her purse and handed them to me.

One was a tax form listing her winnings and the tax due. The second was the bill from the fertility clinic for an implantation procedure performed in early August.

"Do you also have an affidavit from the man you claim to have had an affair with saying you didn't?"

"Of course not. I only told you that so you'd be jealous. But you didn't care, did you." Her eyes were welling with tears that I tried my best to ignore.

"I'm going to need child support from you. After all, you are the biological father."

"I'm not providing support without a custody agreement."

She blinked. Obviously, she hadn't been expecting that. Nor had I. The news that the babies were mine was still sinking in and the words had simply popped out.

She shook her head. "I'll fight you on that, Darren. Unless you marry me."

"Not going to happen." My thoughts about the situation might be a confused jumble, but that one thought was perfectly clear.

She glared at me. "I'll make sure you can't afford to marry anyone else."

"Regardless, I'm not marrying you, Lisa. I'm sorry." It was as gentle as I could manage with my emotions reeling as if blasted by high winds.

We sat staring at each other until, finally, she stood and pulled her coat as closed as it would go. I stood as well, opened the door for her, and watched her walk out, feeling as if my world had just tipped on its axis.

Chapter Twenty-Seven

Devi

I arrived at Mac's Saturday morning and was about to get out of my car when I saw the front door to the complex open and Lisa walked out. If I had to define her expression, I would have picked smug.

She walked over to her car and got in without noticing me. With a sense of dread, I waited for her to drive away before getting out and going inside and knocking since I didn't want to barge in on Mac. He opened the door and smiled with obvious relief when he saw it was me.

He offered me a hug, and with a sigh, I stepped into his arms.

After a moment, I stepped back. "I saw Lisa leaving."

"Figured you might have. I've been avoiding her, so she came here looking for me."

"And?"

"She just lobbed another grenade at me. Come, I think we both need to sit down. If it wasn't so early, I'd break out the Scotch."

"But not to celebrate, I take it?" Not like the other evening. The grim expression on Mac's face erased my smile at that memory.

"Lord, no. Well, I don't know, exactly. There hasn't been time for it to settle in yet."

"What is it?"

Mac sat kitty-corner from me at the table, and reached for my hands, gripping them between his. "She came to tell me..." He shook his head, as if trying to clear it. "That the twins are mine."

"Yours?" The word croaked out, and it was my turn to shake my head to clear it. I pulled on my hands, but Mac didn't let go.

"Claims she won a lottery prize and used it to have the last of the embryos we'd had frozen implanted."

I sat for a minute, letting it settle in. "But can she do that? Without your permission?"

"They had signed consent forms from before, and I doubt she updated them on her marital status."

"She could be lying, though." I was grasping at straws, and I knew it.

"She showed me a bill from the clinic for the last procedure. But that's not all. She wants child support."

I stared at him, unable to come up with a single word. Here we'd been engaged all of five minutes, and I'd thought between that and being able to live rent-free for a year at the Livingstons', we'd solved our problems.

"Devi, are you okay?"

"Not really."

"Just so you know, neither am I." He sat back, letting go of my hands and rubbing his forehead. "It's getting to be too much, isn't it? I wouldn't blame you one bit if you reconsidered that offer from the Winterford and left town by whatever train, plane, or bus would get you out of here the quickest."

"Is that what you'd do if you were me?"

His shoulders slumped. "I don't know. I can't even figure out what to do as me."

"While you think about it, don't forget. We're engaged. And I'm not giving up on that or on you, so don't you dare give up on yourself."

One thing we'd planned to do today was to go shopping for a ring. I knew Mac couldn't afford anything expensive, but he said he wanted me to have something. Now Lisa had sucked the joy out of our plans.

Instead we ran errands together, had lunch, and then went for a walk in a nearby park. When we returned to the apartment, I needed a nap. We lay together on top of the quilt, his arm around me. Despite being upset at Lisa's latest news, I curled up next to him and quickly fell asleep.

Chapter Twenty-Eight

Josephine

I knew immediately something was wrong when Devi and Mac arrived for dinner. Lill noticed it as well, although neither of us asked what it was. I chewed on that thought all through the meal while we talked about, among other things, the scams-and-cons workshop. Lill told us she'd contacted several retirement communities, and all but one were enthusiastic about hosting us.

Both Mac and Devi said their best times were late afternoon, and Lill said she'd let them know possible dates as soon as she got them set up. I stood to clear the table.

"Wait, Josephine. Mac and I have something to tell you."

Judging from the looks on their faces, I didn't think it could be good news. I sat down and braced myself for whatever it was.

"Mac asked me to marry him, and I said yes."

For a moment, Lill and I sat there with what were probably identical flummoxed expressions.

"Why that's wonderful news," I said. "Isn't it?"

"Of course it is." Devi turned to smile at Mac and looked for the first time like it was wonderful news.

He smiled back at her, but although he was going through the motions, I didn't think his heart was in it.

"What is it? What's wrong?" I demanded.

He and Devi looked at each other and Devi nodded, ceding the floor to Mac.

He sighed. "It's my ex-wife. Turns out, she had another implantation procedure using the remaining embryos we'd had frozen. The babies are mine."

"And she's asking for child support," Devi added.

Lill blinked and shook her head. "Oh my. Can she do that?"

"I suspect she can," Mac said.

"But you didn't give your consent to the implantation. Did you?" I said.

"Not this time. But I'm sure a lawyer will argue I'm as responsible as any man who impregnates a woman, either on purpose or by mistake."

I swallowed around a lump in my throat. Mac and Devi deserved their happy ending. Not this prolonged nightmare.

"What are you going to do?"

"All we can do is wait until the babies are born," Mac said.

Devi was holding his hand, but the look she gave me was full of anguish. It was clear there was something else going on here, but I wasn't going to learn what it was while Mac was present.

~ ~ ~

Devi called on Monday and asked to see me. And if she hadn't called me, I'd planned to call her. She sounded odd, as if she had a cold, and when she arrived, it was clear she was upset. The same upset she'd tried to hide on Saturday?

While she took off her coat, I poured tea. She came and sat across from me, ignoring the tea, which is unlike Devi. She appreciates a good cup of tea as much as I do.

"What's wrong?"

Words tumbled out in an anguished stream. "I never told you, but since the shooting..." Devi raised a face ravaged by grief. "I can't have children."

I got up, took a seat next to her, and put my arm around her. "Does Mac know?"

She nodded. "He said it was a relief. That Lisa trying to get pregnant was what destroyed their marriage. But I see what it means to him to be a father, even though he doesn't."

"What do you mean?"

"He's excited about the babies."

"Did he say that?"

"Of course not. You know Mac. You have to look at what he does. Not what he doesn't say."

"What's he doing then?"

"He told me he can't marry me when all he has to offer are debts and difficulties."

"And you said?" I resisted pointing out that she'd just reported something Mac said rather than something he did.

"I reminded him I was making a good salary, and for the next year, we won't be paying rent. That if we work together, we can pay off his debts and have enough to manage."

"And he didn't like the idea?"

"He doesn't think it's fair that a penny of my money should go to pay for the choices he made with Lisa."

"It isn't fair," I said, testing.

"Little in life is fair," she retorted. "We need to accept that."

Which was true and required no response. "What are you going to do?"

"I don't know."

"I could offer him a loan." And I only suggested a loan because I knew Mac wouldn't accept an outright gift.

She frowned. "I doubt he'd go for that."

"Let me talk to him."

~ ~ ~

I asked Mac to stop by on his day off, saying I once again needed his help. Which wasn't even close to the truth, and no, I didn't feel a bit guilty.

He showed up as arranged Wednesday morning. "What is it you need my help with?" he said as I poured coffee for him and tea for me.

"I asked you here under false pretenses."

"As if that's a first."

We smiled at each other, which I considered a good sign. Mac isn't bouncy but he's always even-tempered and pleasant, and the smile made him look more carefree than he'd looked on Saturday.

"I asked you here to give you an engagement present."

"What about Devi? Shouldn't she be here too?"

"I have a ring I no longer wear that I'd like Devi to have, possibly as her engagement ring. But I wanted to check with you first." I pulled out the jeweler's box and opened it, watching him.

He shook his head. "And how long have you had this ring?"

"The original ring was my grandmother's. It was old-fashioned, so I had the stones reset in a modern setting."

Having observed Devi, I didn't think she'd want a large stone protruding, so I'd picked a filigree design with tiny diamonds accompanying the medium-sized diamond that had, in truth, been my grandmother's.

When Mac didn't speak, doubt rushed in. "Is it too pushy of me? Maybe you have a ring from your grandmother...or your mother?"

"Not to worry. The McElroys don't have vintage pieces of jewelry lying around." His mouth twitched. "Very creative of you, Josephine."

"Thank you, Mac."

He took a sip of coffee.

"So you accept the ring?"

"For sure I can't afford something like this. But you can't keep doing this sort of thing."

"I don't know why not. You and Devi are as dear to me as a son and daughter. And family trumps everything, you know."

"Yes. It does."

We each took sips from our respective cups while I thought about what else I wanted to say.

Deciding, I set my cup down with a click. "Devi told me she can't have children."

He glanced at me and then looked away.

"You need to reassure her. She loves you dearly, but—"

"The situation with Lisa is getting to her," he said.

"No. Well, yes, it is. She's worried that she's standing in the way of you having the family you and Lisa tried so hard for."

"She couldn't be more wrong." But after saying that, he stopped speaking and played with his cup, moving it back and forth. Finally, he looked at me. "What do I do here, Josephine? Any wise words?"

"What do you want to do?"

"I want to live my life with Devi by my side. But I can't turn my back on..." He shuddered and looked away. "Lisa and the babies."

"Of course you can't. You're a good man, Darren McElroy. Unselfish, thoughtful, generous. If you turned your back, you'd doom any future you have with Devi. But you need to talk to her about this. Agree on what role you both want to play in these babies' lives. Then figure out how to do that."

He sighed. "I can't accept the ring. But if Devi is willing to accept it, I'd have no objection."

"I'll ask her."

"Thanks, Josephine." He stood and then he leaned over and kissed me on the cheek. The same cheek Norman kissed. I seem to be having a run of men kissing me lately. Can't say I'm not enjoying it, though.

After Mac left, I realized I'd forgotten to mention the loan. But I suspect he would have turned that down as well.

Chapter Twenty-Nine

Lillian

Edna stopped me after dinner and asked if she could come see me, and we set a time for the next morning. She arrived, breathless.

"I just finished my morning walk. Here, I wanted to show you how I'm doing." She handed me a sheet of writing. Not only were her lines trending up, her letters were beginning, here and there, to take on a forward slant.

"Did you notice this?" I pointed at the words that had letters slanting to the right.

Frowning, she leaned over the page while I got up and dug out the sample of her writing from our previous meeting, which I'd kept. The two samples were strikingly different.

"See how your letters are beginning to slant forward?"

"Is that good?"

"Very good. That was the next thing I wanted you to practice, but it looks like you're already well on your way with that. Did you find this difficult to do?"

"Indeed I did. It surprised me. I thought it would be simple. But you were right. I'd get a line or two written, then the next lines would start slanting down. I had to use the ruled lines for over two weeks."

"And how are you feeling?"

Edna cocked her head. "At first, I was really uncomfortable, on edge, you know. But now I have more energy. And I'm more hopeful things can get better."

"I thought when I didn't hear from you, you'd given up."

"No, not at all. I just didn't think I'd made enough progress. But now I'm ready for another suggestion."

"You can focus on slanting your letters to the right."

"Since I'm already doing that, is there anything else?"

I hesitated, but then decided not to lessen her obvious enthusiasm. "Do you see how cramped your writing looks?"

I pointed at several words where the letters bumped up against each other. "You can try expanding your letters and leaving more space."

When she frowned, I grabbed a blank sheet of paper and wrote *Edna Prisant* with the letters cramped together and then I wrote it more expansively.

"I see." Her tone was thoughtful. "Is there anything else?"

"That's more than enough for now. Remember how difficult it was to change the slant of your lines. That was easy compared to this." I pointed at her name written the two different ways. "You know, it might make it easier if you write the same line over and over."

"Like we used to make our students do: 'I will not sass the teacher' one hundred times."

We smiled at each other, one of the few times I could remember smiling at Edna.

"Exactly like that," I said. "If you do what we've talked about, you'll be a different person, you know. You need to get used to that before tackling anything more."

"You ought to give a talk about this, Lillian. I'm sure there are others who'd like to improve their characters and would like to know how to get started."

"But are they willing to do the hard work?"

"Maybe not, but it can't hurt to let them know there's something they can do. And I'd be happy to offer a testimonial."

Edna left then, and I sat mulling over what she'd accomplished so far. For one thing, her outlook had shifted away from the complete me-orientation she'd had up to now. Her suggestion about helping others proved that.

Chapter Thirty

Josephine

I called Philippa and invited her for afternoon tea. I'd decided that as an ex-attorney, she might be able to shed some light on the situation between Mac and Lisa. And yes, I knew I was sticking my nose in much further than was wise.

But an informal consult with a friend as the source of information...what could it hurt?

"Do you prefer white, green, or black tea?" I asked after Philippa had taken a seat on my sofa.

"Please, you choose."

I went to the kitchen and brewed a pot of green tea. When I returned to the living room, Philippa was standing in front of my Demeri painting.

"I've never heard of this artist, but I like this painting. Amazing the complex effect he managed with only pale blues and white."

"Yes. It's supposed to be a dream scene. And that's where I had the Hopper hanging, by the way. I kept people out so no one would know it was there. Unfortunately, it didn't work."

"I heard it was your son who gave the game away?"

"He did."

"Where's the painting now?"

"The Cincinnati Art Museum is storing it. They'll be hanging it in a public gallery shortly."

"I'm sorry you couldn't keep it here."

"Yes, so am I. But my son tried to use its presence as proof I was incompetent to manage my own affairs."

Her eyebrows shot up. "He obviously didn't succeed."

"He came close enough to give me a good scare."

We both took sips of our tea, and I handed Philippa a plate of Servatii's cookies.

"This tea is delicious." Philippa took a cookie and handed the plate back to me.

"It's a new one my tea broker just found for me."

"Tea broker?"

"He lives in Taiwan. I met him years ago when he was in Cincinnati on a student exchange program. He discovered I liked tea, and he's been expanding my palate ever since."

Philippa took another sip. "He sells tea?"

"Yes, he has a website. Treasure Tea Leaves dot com."

"I'll have to check it out."

"If you'd like to order something, let me know and I'll add it to my next order to minimize the shipping."

"Thank you. I'll do that."

I set my cup down with a decisive click. "I confess I had an ulterior motive for inviting you today."

"What's that?"

"I'm hoping you'll be willing to put your attorney hat back on long enough to tell me what you think about something."

"About you and your son?"

I shook my head. "I believe I have that under control. No, what I want to ask you about involves a friend who's in a difficult circumstance, and I'd like a better idea what he's facing in legal terms." I then outlined what was happening between Mac and Lisa.

"And your specific question is?"

"Does he have a chance of getting joint custody?"

"This is the new frontier in family law," she said. "IVF, surrogacy, sperm banks. I'm afraid I'm not up on all that since I haven't practiced in over ten years. However, for what it's worth, in my opinion, since they created the embryos while they were married, the man would have an excellent basis on which to request joint custody. The best strategy, though, would be for him to work this out with the woman privately. How antagonistic was the divorce? Do you know?"

"I don't know. But the woman recently moved in with him when she hit a rough financial patch. So I assume they originally parted on decent terms."

"Are they still living together?"

"No." I debated whether to say more, then decided if I didn't, Philippa wouldn't have all the information she needed to advise me. "The man is in another relationship."

"And the ex-wife knows this?"

"Yes. But she's telling people she's still married to him."

"Uh-oh. Well, I can see one scenario developing here. If the ex-wife is angry about the husband's moving on, that might be why she's saying she'll fight him over custody."

I hadn't thought of that angle, but now that Philippa had voiced it, I could see how obvious it was that Lisa could be acting vindictively. "Thank you. That's very helpful."

"I'm glad. But I didn't have any specific advice for you."

"But you've given me an idea for a way around the problem." I gestured at her cup, and when she nodded, I refilled it. "And how are you settling in? No more naked poker run-ins? At least, none I've heard about."

"No, I've been busy writing, and you know what? I have you to thank for that. The naked poker game and the story about your Hopper painting got my creative juices flowing."

"I'm glad to hear it. I think."

"Not to worry. I'm giving it all kinds of twists. You won't recognize it once I'm finished. You see, I always start with a tiny little 'what if.' But it soon develops a life of its own."

"I love to read, and I've often wondered where writers get their ideas."

"Mostly out of thin air. It also helps if you like to daydream and don't mind spending lots of time alone."

"Well, I've certainly got that time-alone part down pat."

We smiled at each other and continued to sip tea.

Chapter Thirty-One

Devi

At Josephine's request, I stopped by Brookside on my way home from work.

"How are the new digs working out?" she asked after I settled on the couch with a cup of tea in my hands and my feet tucked beneath me. It might be the first of March, but it was bitterly cold out, and my car heater hadn't put out warm air until I was almost to Brookside.

"It's great. But I can hardly wait until the Livingstons leave and Mac can move in."

"Do you know if he's told Lisa about the move?"

"I don't believe he has. He talks to her as little as possible. You see, he's moved out of the house and into my old apartment to get away from her."

"Have they talked any more about the child support and custody issues?"

"I don't know for sure. But I don't think he's seen her since she told him the babies were his."

"Good. Because I have something for him to think about."

I wondered why she wasn't telling Mac, although I was more than willing to listen to any ideas. I knew Josephine was just itching to wave her magic money wand to solve the problem of Lisa. But I also knew Mac and I needed to work through how to respond without a fairy godmother.

"What I'm thinking," Josephine said, "is that it's possible you're the reason Lisa's saying she'll fight him on the custody issue."

"I don't understand."

"You said she's telling her work colleagues they're still married, so it makes perfect sense she'd be jealous of you and want to make Mac pay for being with you instead of her. So I think it makes sense for you two to separate."

I couldn't believe what I was hearing. "You're saying I should break up with him?"

"No. No. Well, not for real. But what if you and Mac did some pretending of your own?"

"Ah, you're saying we should pretend to break up." The idea, which at first seemed outlandish, on second thought had a certain symmetry.

"Yes. Exactly. Then Mac can suggest a compromise with Lisa over custody and support. And since, from what you've said, Lisa doesn't have the money to fight it out in court..."

"That's for sure." I sighed. "But I don't know if they're getting along well enough to negotiate."

"Then maybe they need a mediator." Josephine leaned toward me, obviously caught up by her suggestion. "Did you know Philippa used to be an attorney?"

"I thought she was an author."

"Attorney first, author second. And I bet she'd consider taking this on as book research, but you have to be the one to sell it to Mac."

I stared out the window where snowflakes were lazily falling. Josephine, who has excellent instincts about when not to push, left me alone to think. At some point, she left the room. Then she came and sat back down.

"There's another reason I wanted to see you," she said.

I turned my gaze from falling snow to the woman sitting across from me. She looked intent, her hands clenched in her lap.

"I spoke with Mac last week to get his approval," she said.

"For what?"

"Well..." Her gaze dropped, and she caught her lip between her teeth, looking uncertain. "I know you have a mom and grandmothers, but I hope for a few minutes you'll consider me an honorary grandmother."

"And a very, very dear friend," I said, beginning to worry. "What is it, Josephine?"

"As an honorary grandmother, I want to give you my blessing on your engagement. And I also want to give you an heirloom that belonged to my grandmother."

She opened her hand, which held a diamond ring that looked modern to me.

"Josephine." I shook my head. "If that's an heirloom, I'm a unicorn."

She shrugged and smiled. "The original setting was old-fashioned, so I had the stones reset. I thought you'd like this better."

"It's gorgeous. And you say Mac approved?"

"He said he couldn't accept it, but that he had no objection to you accepting it. And I would be so honored if you would."

"Didn't you just advise me to break up with him?"

"I doubt you and Mac will have to pretend to be separated for long."

"Oh, I hope not," I said with a sigh.

Chapter Thirty-Two

Mac

When Devi first suggested that Lisa might be opposing my request for joint custody because of jealousy, I rejected the idea. I also dismissed Devi's accompanying suggestion I tell Lisa we'd broken up, although I kept both thoughts to myself because Devi has been incredibly understanding of the situation with Lisa, and I didn't think it was fair to make any part of it more difficult for her than it already was.

But after thinking about her comments, I decided they were worth considering. And so I called Lisa and asked if I could stop by.

"What for?"

"We need to talk."

"About?"

"The last time I saw you, didn't you say something about my providing financial support? Well, I want to talk to you about it."

"I'm really tired tonight. Why don't you come over Saturday morning. But not too early."

"Okay. I'll see you Saturday." Which was good, because it meant I could take Teddy and Bruno for a walk. Since I'd moved out and been avoiding Lisa, I'd not seen the two, and I missed them.

~ ~ ~

On Saturday, Kate greeted me with a hug. "Mac, we've really missed you."

At her words, Teddy and Bruno both came barreling out of the kitchen, Teddy to throw his arms around my knees, and Bruno to swipe his tongue over whatever part of my anatomy was handy, which mostly translated into hands and face.

"Are you up for a walk?" I asked Teddy.

"Yeth," he shouted while Bruno made the peculiar whooping noise that is his version of a bark.

"I wondered what was happening with you," Kate said, pulling Teddy's coat out of the closet.

"Where were you, Mac?" Teddy demanded, forgetting to speak slowly.

"I've been staying in Devi's apartment," I told Kate. "She's house-sitting."

As we talked, she got Teddy into his coat and then turned him so she could zip him up while I stuffed each of his hands into a mitten and pulled a hat over his ears.

"I won't keep him out too long. I need to speak to Lisa when I get back."

"She's been over here a couple of times." Kate's tone made a question of it. "Last time, she seemed annoyed about something to do with you. Asked me questions about who you were seeing. I told her as little as possible."

"Sorry she's been bothering you." I knelt to snap on Bruno's leash. His claws scrabbled for purchase on the hardwood floor as he pulled me toward the door. "Talk later," I told Kate.

It was a relief to be outside in the cold, clear morning. We walked to the memorial circle, where there were statues of soldiers from a variety of conflicts. And then, for the first time since the shooting, I took Teddy to Servatii's for a cup of cocoa and a doughnut.

While he ate and drank, I held a cup of coffee, lost in memory and rarely remembering to take a sip. Bruno lay outside the door like he had the last time we were here. He'd snuffled around the spot where he and Devi lay after being shot, finally flopping down, his head on his paws, his usual mournful look in place.

He obviously had memories of what happened here. But if his thought processes could handle the complexity, he knew Devi was okay since she'd insisted on going to see him after she got out of the hospital, accompanied by juicy bones and a super-sized bag of Bruno's favorite treats.

Teddy, on the other hand, seemed not to remember any of what happened. But then the woman who waited on us that day had hustled him into the back when the shooting started, so he'd seen little. I was glad of it. Teddy's such a happy kid; I don't want anything to make him fearful.

When Teddy had finished both cocoa and doughnut, we walked back to his house, and then, accompanied by a hefty dose of trepidation, I went next door and knocked. Lisa came to the door still wearing a robe and with her hair uncombed, even though she was expecting me and it was after ten.

"Don't know why you bothered to knock," she said, sounding irritable. "It's your house."

I bit off my immediate ill-advised response, which would have been, "not anymore."

She walked in front of me to the kitchen, looking heavy and awkward, her hand pressed to the small of her back. She pointed at the coffeepot and, sighing, took a seat in the other chair.

"How are you feeling?" In the short time since I last saw her, she'd doubled in size. Well, that was probably an exaggeration. But for sure, she was noticeably larger.

"Exhausted," she said.

"How much longer are you planning to teach?"

She shrugged. "As long as possible since being busy takes my mind off how uncomfortable I'm feeling. So, you're here to talk about supporting your son and daughter?"

The words sank in and I began to smile.

"Easy for you," Lisa grumbled, pushing hair behind her ear, only to have it flop forward again. She looked like she'd just gotten out of bed. It was a look I used to love. Tumbled hair, rosy cheeks, lips curved in a smile. That had morphed today to tumbled hair, circles under her eyes, and lips pressed together as if in pain.

"Tell me your thinking," I said, not needing to fake the sympathy I was feeling.

She shrugged. "It will cost most of my salary for just an apartment and day care. That means I'll have practically nothing left to pay for everything else."

Her statement confirmed my own conclusions, and what she needed from me was clear, without her spelling it out further. I wondered if she'd thought about any of this before deciding to use her lottery win to get pregnant. Not that it would be helpful to bring that question up.

"You're only asking me for money, but I want the chance to be a father."

Her head jerked up. "You mean marry me?"

I shook my head. "That's not going to work for us, Lisa."

"Because you have Whatshername and a life?" The words were furious and an angry expression pulled her face tight, giving a hint of what she'd look like as an old woman.

In the silence that followed, I thought about Devi's advice. I couldn't outright lie to Lisa, but there just might be another way.

"What if I told you that was over," I said.

"Aren't you living with her?"

"No. I'm not." Not yet, at any rate.

"But I saw you there, in her apartment. With your toiletries in the bathroom and your clothes and everything. So don't lie to me."

"It's true, I'm staying in her apartment. But she's moved out. I told her the babies were mine and that you'd asked for support, and she...well, you saw for yourself she wasn't living there."

"Couldn't wait to get out of Dodge, huh?" The angry look softened into a satisfied smirk.

"Something like that." It was exhausting, trying to come up with responses that weren't outright lies, but which twisted the truth enough to convince Lisa that Devi and I had called it quits. "You were right, Lisa. About me wanting children as much as you do. And now...well, I want to both help you and be part of their lives. Surely you can understand and accept that after all we went through."

She sat back, fingering her coffee cup, and I noticed she was still wearing the fake wedding ring. I wondered how long it would be before I could place a ring on Devi's finger and whether she'd continue to want me, with Lisa and two children firmly embedded in my life. Because that was where this was going.

As Lisa cocked her head and stared at me, I looked back, knowing I'd given it my best shot and now it was out of my hands.

"Okay. How do we do this?" she said.

"You're willing to grant me joint custody?"

She stilled, but then her posture eased. "Maybe, but only if you agree to pay half the twins' expenses."

"It would be better to settle on a fixed amount." I didn't think I could face the detailed accounting and subsequent wrangling that would ensue if we didn't do it that way.

She lifted her chin in challenge and named an amount that was more than half my salary. And she knew it.

Then I remembered what else Devi had suggested. "How about we work with a mediator on the specifics?"

"Who pays for that?"

"I will. I know an attorney who might be willing to do it."

"Humph. And that person would be on your side from the get-go, right?"

"It's someone I'm acquainted with, but I don't know her well. If she's willing to take it on, you could meet with her. See if she's acceptable. If she's not, then we'll find someone else."

Lisa sat there for a time, her mouth going through a number of contortions as if she were chewing on words and getting ready either to swallow them or to spit them out.

"Okay. But I have to meet her, and I'll be the one to decide if she's acceptable."

"I'll call to set something up," I said, standing.

She nodded, her eyes filling with tears. I turned to leave, pretending I hadn't noticed.

"You better not be lying to me, Darren. About any of it."

On that unhappy note, I walked out, closing the door carefully.

Driving away, I knew I needed to do two things. Figure out what level of support I could afford, and talk to Philippa.

I also knew, until I had Lisa's signature on an agreement, I couldn't take the risk of being seen with Devi. She couldn't even come to the apartment, since Lisa knew where that was and had already shown a tendency for dropping in unannounced.

And telling Devi that and then living with the reality was going to be difficult.

Chapter Thirty-Three

Josephine

"I thought I'd stop by to let you know tomorrow's my last day," Norman said.

"Yes, I know."

"I did try to talk them out of a party."

"Everyone is fond of you. They want to wish you well."

"You didn't tell anyone what I was really doing here?"

"I told Lill, but if I'd wanted everyone to know, I would have told Myrtle."

Norman chuckled. "Myrtle is quite the chatty belle, isn't she?"

"I'm sure she's devastated you're leaving. Although she took up with Bertie again the moment she heard."

"And what about you, Jo? Any devastation there?"

"What a remarkably unchivalrous query, Mr. Neumann."

"You're right. Especially since I'm here to explain why I haven't asked you out again. It's because I enjoyed your company too much to maintain a believable facade with the Myrtles of the world. But now that I'll no longer be in that uncomfortable position, I'd very much like to take you to dinner."

"Do you think we'll have anything to talk about now that you no longer suspect me?"

"I doubt that will be a problem."

"I need to give it some thought."

"How much time for reflection are we talking about?"

"You may call me next week."

"All right. I'll do that, Maggie." And before I could challenge him for calling me Maggie instead of Jo, he'd turned and walked away.

Maggie, indeed. As in Maggie Smith, aka the dowager countess of Grantham, I suspected. But then I had taken a page from Maggie's playbook to express my annoyance with Norman for taking me to dinner and then ignoring me with no explanation for nearly a week.

Startling to realize my frustration over that was identical to what I'd felt in high school when something similar happened. And my reaction today—not immediately accepting the invitation—had its roots in high school as well. Not an easy thing to admit at my age.

~ ~ ~

Lill insisted we attend Norman's going-away party, although it had been my firm intention not to.

"Never pass up a chance to party, Josephine," Lill said. "At our age, who knows how many more candles we'll get to blow out?"

"I don't believe candles are involved. It's not his birthday after all."

"You know exactly what I'm saying. Now, change into something pretty and let's party."

"I could make other friends."

"No, you couldn't." Lill sounded smug. "You're stuck with me. Chop-chop."

Resigned, I changed into a pair of slacks and added a jacket, and Lill proclaimed me acceptable.

"Norman asked me to dinner again," I told her as we walked to the community room.

"What? When?"

"Yesterday."

"And?"

"I haven't decided if I'm accepting yet."

"Josephine Bartlett. If you don't tell that man you'll go to dinner with him, I will. And then you can find yourself a new friend."

"That's certainly supportive."

"Okay. You want supportive? Then tell me why you're holding back."

"I-I like being on my own. Since Thomas died, it's like I've been let out of prison. And I don't want to give that up."

"For Pete's sake, Josephine. It's only dinner."

"It's another step along a road I've no interest in traveling. Better to nip it in the bud than to string him along."

"I don't know why I'm surprised. You have the most obvious caution strokes I've ever come across. They're even more pronounced than Mac's."

"Caution strokes? What are you talking about?"

"Your handwriting."

"You analyzed my handwriting?"

"I've been worried about you, so I thought I'd take a quick peek. After all, you suggested Graphotherapy for Edna, so why not give it a try yourself? I can show you the change you need to make. It's a simple one, although that doesn't mean it'll be easy."

We both stopped walking and stood looking at each other.

"What do I do?" I said.

"After the party, come with me and I'll show you. And I have one other suggestion."

"Of course you do."

"You could lay it out for Norman. What you want; what you don't want. Maybe he wants the same thing you do."

"He could want my money."

"Really? You think that, do you?"

"It's not unheard of." Although, in Norman's case, it was unlikely. The background check had revealed he was comfortably off. But then some people never seem to have enough.

Lill shook her head. "If that's what you think, then best to steer clear."

"Isn't that what I've been saying?"

And on that note, we arrived at the community room to take our places at the end of the line of people shuffling forward to tell Norman good-bye.

When my turn came, I stepped up to him and offered him my hand.

"Jo," he said, his smile growing wider. "I was afraid you weren't coming."

"She wasn't," Lill offered over my right shoulder. "I made her."

"Is that true?" He was still holding my hand, and I seemed to have lost the power to pull free.

When I didn't answer, he cocked his head. "To be continued." He let go of me and turned to Lill, who stepped up and hugged him.

She whispered something in his ear that made him grin. Then she propelled me over to the cake table. But if I ate a piece of cake at every Brookside party, I'd quickly need to supersize my wardrobe. Lill, who always indulges, is as skinny as a coat hanger.

"Got those good genes working for me, and I'm not talking denim," she said the one time I commented on it.

Candace was helping to serve the cake, something she avoids whenever she can. But with Norman leaving and Devi not coming back, she has to carry out duties she normally, and quite happily, delegates to others.

Once everyone had a piece of cake, there were awkward speeches, one by Candace and a second by Myrtle, supplemented by comments from our more extroverted residents. After that, the party settled into the usual torpor.

Norman moved around the room, talking to everyone. I watched him as I reduced a piece of cake to crumbs, still trying to decide if I wanted to spend more time with him. Clearly, he was an extrovert while I was the opposite. He could drive me mad. On the other hand, I had enjoyed talking to him.

He's intelligent and widely read. Two essential characteristics that had also attracted me to Daniel.

Remembering Daniel ended any temptation to eat the cake.

"Demolishing, are we?" Lill waved her fork at me. "This tastes like one of Clara's cakes. Take one bite and you'll be hooked."

"Which is a good reason not to even start." I laid my fork down and pushed the plate farther out of reach.

"Just like Norman might be delicious, so better to leave him untasted as well?" Lill said, her eyebrows arching.

"I don't think I'd put it quite that way. But I suppose you're right. Better to have never tasted than be left craving more."

"Has that happened to you, Josephine?"

Lill's serious look made my stomach do a flip-flop.

"I had more than enough of Thomas to last three lifetimes," I said, deliberately misunderstanding her.

"I wasn't talking about Thomas, and you know it. But did you ever give your heart to someone and have it broken?"

"Of course. Doesn't everybody?"

"No. I don't believe everybody does. I think some people sail through life not caring enough for anyone besides themselves to have their hearts touched. But I don't think you're one of them."

"No. I don't think I am. And that's more than enough of that. Here, you can have my piece." I pushed the plate toward her.

"It would be a sin to waste one of Clara's creations," Lill said, licking frosting off her fork. Clara is the chef hired by the new manager. Together, they've had a positive impact on the quality of the Brookside experience.

As Lill ate the second piece of cake, I looked around. Across the room, I saw Myrtle reach out and grab Norman's hand and then hold on to it while she fluttered her eyelashes at him.

The sight gave me a slight pain.

Lill looked up and saw what I was looking at. "Norman and Myrtle." She shook her head. "I'll bet you he's never asked her to dinner."

"Who asked who?" Philippa said. "Can I join you?"

"Please do," Lill said. "I was just saying that I doubt Norman ever had any interest in Myrtle. Don't you agree?"

Philippa shrugged. "Doubtful." She took a bite of cake. "Umm. Guess I'll have to put in an extra thirty minutes on the treadmill tomorrow. But this is definitely worth it."

"I'm leaving before I'm tempted," I said, standing.

"By the cake?" Lill gave me one of her *Lill* looks.

"Of course, by the cake."

"And I'll see you later?" Lill said.

"Sure. Fine."

I checked to find that Myrtle had Norman trapped, but somehow as I reached the door, he was there to usher me through.

"About dinner?" he said.

"Pick me up at six." I decided Lill's suggestion I spell things out for Norman was a good one. I didn't hesitate or slow down, though, so I had no idea how he responded. I guessed I'd find out at six.

I didn't have time to work up to a nervous state because a few minutes later Lill knocked on my door, marched in, and sat me down. She pulled out a copy of what I'd written for the inspiration book we'd put together in the autumn and showed me what a caution stroke was.

"See these marks here at the end of your sentences? Lill pointed with the tip of her pencil. Once I knew what to look for, I could see them easily.

"Here, try to write some lines, but don't add that stroke." Lill handed me the pencil and a fresh sheet of paper.

The quick red fox caught the slow March hare, I wrote, for no discernable reason. I added the period at the end and found my pen seemingly on its own adding the stroke Lill called a caution stroke. Clearly it was going to take concentration not to add it.

"It's harder to do than it sounds." I sat back, a feeling of frustration washing over me.

Lill patted me on the arm. "You need to take it slow, Josephine. You've probably been cautious a very long time. So work on it, but only if you decide you want to change."

"If I decide to try, what do I need to do?"

152

"Every day for at least a month write out a page, concentrating on eliminating the caution strokes. Then keep track of how you feel. Don't push too hard. Stop if it makes you uncomfortable."

"Is that what you have Edna doing?"

"Yes. Well, different strokes, of course."

"And it's working for her?"

"I think so. She came back for more advice. And she said she felt more optimistic."

"That is a change."

Edna had also replaced the bland polyester pantsuits that had been her wardrobe staple. Now she wore colors that sometimes rivaled Myrtle's outfits.

"Do you want to be less cautious?" For once, Lill's expression was serious.

"I...I'm not sure." After all, I could no longer remember what it was like not being cautious, although I assumed there must have been a time when I hadn't been.

"Well, if you decide you want to change, you know what to do."

"Yes. Okay. Thank you."

~ ~ ~

At six, there was a knock on my door. I opened it to find Norman leaning on the jamb.

"You did mean tonight?" he said, straightening.

I nodded, my mouth drying out. "Let me get my coat."

He stood waiting as I pulled on my coat and picked up my purse, then he walked me out to his car, a sedate silver Mercedes.

"Not as distinctive a choice as your car," he'd said with a grin the first time he took me to dinner.

After opening the door for me, he walked around to the driver's side. "I'm glad you said yes to tonight. What with it being my last day at Brookside, I was feeling at loose ends."

"Don't you and your partner have cases you're working on?"

"We do." He sighed. "You know, I've enjoyed getting away from all that for a while. It's made me think I should consider retiring."

"And do what?"

"I'm not entirely sure. But I've enjoyed myself at Brookside. After being on my own five years, it was nice having so many people to interact with every day."

"I'm sure Candace would be happy to give you your job back."

"No longer a viable option, since there are rules about relationships between staff and residents."

"I don't understand."

"I doubt Candace would approve of us dating."

"Dating?" My voice cracked and I had to clear my throat.

"Us spending time together then," he said with a quick glance and a frown.

"I think we need to talk about that."

"Okay." He shrugged and glanced at me again. "Maybe we could wait until we have glasses of wine in front of us?"

"Yes. That's probably best."

"Of course, that leaves us with empty air to fill since we aren't even at the restaurant yet."

"Yes. Well. Maybe you could tell me about some of your cases?"

"And you can tell me the real story behind the Hopper."

Not going to happen. "Cases first." I crossed my fingers at the lie, even though it was an indirect one.

When Norman started talking, I discovered that among his talents was the skill to tell a story well, which is rarer than you might think. Most people stuff their stories with irrelevant details, and then go back and forth to make sure everything is organized precisely in the order it happened and all the names are correct. As a result, it often becomes tedious waiting for them to get to the point. None of that was true of Norman's story about how he and his partner helped recover a painting that no one knew was missing for three years because a copy had replaced it.

"The forger was vastly relieved to turn the original over to us. You see, he'd replaced it on a lark, but then the museum improved their security and he couldn't switch the paintings back."

"Was he prosecuted?"

"The museum declined to press charges. They didn't want it publicized that they'd been duped for so long by a copy. The forger now consults with museums on preventing similar losses."

By the time Norman finished the story, we were seated and glasses of wine had been placed in front of us.

He saluted me with his glass, then took a sip. "Okay, Jo. Your turn. The Hopper?"

"I've already told you the story. Just a lucky bit of serendipity that I happened upon it at a time when I could afford to buy it." I smiled in a way I hoped conveyed that was all I cared to share before changing the subject. "Actually, what I want to talk about is our spending time together. I'm not sure it's such a good idea."

Norman blinked and set his glass down without taking another sip. "Why not?"

"It's a first step to becoming involved. And I have no interest in being involved with you. Or, for that matter, anyone."

"Because?"

"See, here's the problem. I'm relieved to be on my own. I like the quiet. The peace. I like that I get to decide what kind of furniture to have, which paintings to hang. If I want to listen to music, I get to pick what to listen to. Same with shows on television. I control the remote, and I don't have to take into account anyone's tastes but my own."

Norman sat back and nodded at me. "You said your husband didn't share. I take it he also didn't concern himself with what you might have wanted versus what he wanted."

"Why do you say that?"

"Because everything you've mentioned would be trivial to someone who's cared for. Had your husband shared those choices with you, I doubt being in control would be so important now that you'd preemptively turn down an offer of friendship."

"You may be right. But that doesn't alter the basic situation."

"So you're saying you'd rather stop seeing me than see if we could be friends?"

I nodded.

"Because that would be a real shame. And someday I hope to remind you of this conversation and laugh about it. With you."

"That's unlikely, isn't it?"

"At the moment, it appears so. But somehow I think you're more courageous than that."

"No. I don't think I am."

He sat staring at me, and I struggled with where to look and what to do with my hands.

Finally he spoke. "I was married for forty years to a woman I loved dearly. During that time, I never looked at another woman. Not even when I was away for weeks at a time working a case. I always hoped we'd be one of those lucky couples who live long, happy lives and die of old age within minutes of each other. Obviously, that's not what happened."

I picked up my wine in a vain attempt to hide behind the glass, but found I didn't need that barrier, because while he spoke, Norman was looking off into the distance. He may have even momentarily forgotten I was there.

Then he gave himself a shake and looked back at me. "I never expected to meet someone. Actually, I never tried. Dating sites." He shuddered, and I did too.

"Anyway, I've met a lot of people in my sixty-nine years. But I never felt...I didn't think there could be another person I'd enjoy being with the way I did Beth. Then I met you. You're funny, interesting, bright as all get-out. I like talking to you, and I like that you share when we eat out."

"You aren't interested in me because I own a Hopper?" Might as well put all the cards on the table.

He blinked, then smiled. "It's true that was the original reason for my interest. But not anymore."

The waiter bringing our salads interrupted us. Funny, I didn't think I'd be able to eat, but Norman had managed to turn things around, and I discovered I was hungry.

While I took a bite, I thought about what being friends with Norman might mean long-term. "While Thomas, my husband, was alive, I had to hide who I was and what I was capable of."

He frowned. "Why?"

"He would have taken whatever he could. He did take it all, once. Then I set up a corporation. But it was exhausting, hiding from him. Then when he died, I learned he'd moved most of our assets into a joint account with our son, Jeff."

Norman's fork remained suspended. "Shifting his control of you to Jeff."

"Yes." I didn't know why I was telling Norman all of this. But although I didn't think it was the right thing to do, I couldn't seem to stop talking. "When Jeff learned I had substantial assets of my own, he tried to have me declared mentally incompetent so he could take them over."

Norman set his fork down, leaned his elbows on the table, and clenched his hands but said nothing.

"So you see, I'm not interested in giving anyone, man or woman, control over me ever again."

He sighed and looked away, obviously turning over what I'd told him in his head. Then he shook his head and looked back at me.

"Thank you for telling me all that, Jo. It helps me understand why you feel the way you do. And if it's your decision not to see me again?" He paused and glanced at me. I nodded.

"Then I accept that, and I won't bother you. But if you ever change your mind, you'll let me know?"

After a moment, I nodded again. He picked up his fork and resumed eating as if we'd just been discussing something unimportant, like the weather. Or the Bengals.

I took a bite, looking for a way to change the subject. "So. What cases are you working on now?"

Norman played along, and it eased us through our entrees. I said *no, thank you* to dessert, and Norman drove me back to Brookside and walked me to my door. He didn't kiss me on the cheek, and I didn't invite him in for a nightcap.

When I closed the door after saying good-night, I didn't expect to ever see him again.

Chapter Thirty-Four

Philippa

We took the scams-and-cons workshop on the road, and as we were waiting for the audience to get settled, Mac asked if he could speak with me when we finished. He appeared grave, and his request left me worrying there might be an official aspect to our conversation, although I had no idea what it might be.

I tried not to let myself be distracted by those thoughts as he and I went through our scenes. It was my first time doing the jury-summons scene, but with Norman gone, Lillian had asked me to take it on. I'd been surprised when Norman didn't join us since he'd said at his going-away party he'd still like to be involved with the workshop.

"He's busy working on a case," Lillian said with a frown. She looked pointedly at Josephine, who refused to look back.

The performance went well, and a lively discussion followed. When that wrapped up, our audience surrounded us, shaking our hands and thanking us. As the crowd thinned, I looked over at Mac, and he gestured with his head to meet him out front.

"Will this take long? I came with Josephine," I told him.

"Probably better to let her know I'm giving you a ride back. If that's okay?"

I said it was, and when I told Josephine Mac wanted to talk to me and would give me a ride back to Brookside, her response was an emphatic, "Good."

That puzzled me until Mac described his problem. We'd driven to a nearby Panera, and the situation he was asking me about duplicated the "friend's" situation Josephine had described.

"Josephine suggested we use a mediator, and she said you might be willing to consider doing it? I'd pay you, of course."

"I am interested, but if I do it, it will be pro bono."

"I prefer to pay."

From the look on his face, I judged him unlikely to budge on the point. "Okay. I do mediations for a flat rate. Three hundred dollars." Which was what I used to charge for a single hour of my time when I was practicing law, but I hoped it was enough to satisfy Mac's need to pay.

"I mentioned the possibility of mediation to Lisa, and she's willing to consider it. But she wants to meet you before she decides. She's concerned since you already know me, you'll be prejudiced on my behalf."

"It's a valid concern since I have a favorable opinion of you. And although it's my aim to be unbiased in a mediation, we all know that's an ideal few humans can achieve."

"Okay. So, what do we do next?"

"I need to speak with Lisa. If she finds me acceptable, great. If not, I can suggest someone who doesn't know either of you."

He called me later to set up a Saturday afternoon meeting with Lisa, for which I reserved one of the small sitting rooms at Brookside.

~ ~ ~

On Saturday, Lisa, I knew it had to be her, paused in the doorway before stepping into the room and extending a hand to me. I gestured for her to take a seat. Her pregnancy made her move awkwardly, but despite that, she had the look of someone who'd been the head cheerleader and homecoming queen in high school.

To prevent further bias on my part, I'd stopped Mac from giving me details about their relationship. But now I found myself curious about them.

"This is your meeting, Lisa," I told her. "I expect you have questions for me?"

"I do. How well do you know Darren?"

It took me a beat to realize she was referring to Mac.

"Not that well. I met him only recently when we were putting together the scams-and-cons workshop."

She gave me a puzzled look, and I remembered Josephine saying she didn't know how much Mac and Lisa were talking to each other. I explained about the workshop.

"And what do you think of Darren?"

"I believe he's a conscientious police officer."

"Do you like him?"

"I don't know him well enough to give a definitive answer to that, but I do have a positive impression of him."

"What's your impression of me?"

"That you're direct and obviously well-educated."

"Do you like directness in a woman?"

"I do. It's one of my ambitions, to always be direct."

"Darren said you're no longer a practicing lawyer?"

"I'm still licensed, if that's your question. But I retired ten years ago."

"Why maintain your license then?"

"Because one never knows what life will serve up."

That made her scoff. "So, what do you do with your time now you're retired?"

"I write. Novels."

Lisa sat back, blinking. Then she leaned forward, although her forward movement was impeded by her enlarged belly. "Do you have any children?"

"I do not." No way was I sharing with her my history of miscarriages.

She sat back. "What do you know about Darren and me?"

"I know you got pregnant through the implantation of embryos and that Darren is the biological father of the babies you're carrying. I know you're asking for child support that Darren is willing to provide as long as you agree to a custody arrangement."

Her eyes narrowed. "So, what will your role be?"

"I'll help you with the specific details so that what you agree to is enforceable by the power of the law."

"Will the three of us meet?"

"At some point, yes. But initially, the best approach is for each of you to spell out your positions and allow me to serve as a go-between in settling the specifics."

"Okay. Well, I can do that now."

"Go ahead, then."

"Darren may have joint custody as long as he remains single and keeps up his support payments. And as for those payments." She named a figure, which I noted. "That is, unless there are unexpected medical expenses."

I nodded to indicate I'd heard her. "I need to ask you some background information. Is that all right?"

"Of course."

"Were you awarded any support when you and Darren divorced?"

"No. But he agreed to take on the remaining debt from the *in vitro* treatments."

"Including the one that resulted in your pregnancy?"

"No. I paid for that myself."

"Did Darren consent to that procedure?"

She wiggled and bit her lip. "He consented to the creation of the embryos."

"But not their implantation."

"Only the last two." She glanced up at me, still chewing on her lip.

"And your divorce, what were the grounds?"

"Irreconcilable differences."

"Specifically?"

She took a breath, then hesitated. Another breath and a humph. "I wanted to continue trying to have a baby. He wanted to stop."

"Did he leave you, or did you leave him?"

Her lips firmed, and she looked away. "My intention was to take time off from our marriage. Unfortunately, Darren interpreted it as abandonment."

I sat back and waited to see if she had anything more to say.

She glanced at me. "Well?"

"I see several weaknesses in your position."

"What?"

"You were the one who left the marital home. And you had the embryos implanted without Darren's specific consent. You also need to know it's not possible to make Darren's marital status a requirement for his having custody."

"You're on his side, is that what you're saying?" If she hadn't been pregnant, I think she would have jumped to her feet and paced.

"I'm not on either side, Lisa. My role is to look at both sides, point out weaknesses, and help you to reach an agreement. I haven't yet gotten information from Darren, so I know only the problematic areas on your side of the issue."

"What do you think the problems will be on Darren's side?"

"There's no way I can predict that until I speak to him, and I didn't want to do that unless you considered me suitable."

"Okay. I agree, you're suitable. Now what?"

"I'll talk to him. And I'll get financial information from you both. The type of information you no doubt provided when you divorced."

"I don't see how I can make it on less than what I'm asking for." Her expression hardened into one at odds with the prom-queen image she'd been projecting up to now.

"But you're saying you'll work with me?"

She hesitated. "Yes."

"I'll need to see your financials, then. With specific estimates of your projected expenses." I stopped and smiled at her, hoping to soften her stance before she walked out. "When are you due?"

"May. And it can't come soon enough."

"Then we need to get moving on this."

Mediations, even friendly ones, always take longer than one hopes. And this one had layers of complexity that were likely to take major finessing.

~ ~ ~

After I met with Lisa, she and Mac provided me with their financial data, and shortly after that, I was able to get their agreement, in principle, on the monthly amount Mac would provide for the support of the twins. But they remained deadlocked on the issue of custody.

"I suggest you approach this the way you would have if you'd had children at the time you divorced."

"What does that mean?" Lisa's tone was snappish, probably because she was so obviously uncomfortable.

"It means you would have agreed to a schedule of visitation. For example, some couples arrange it so the children stay with one parent during the week and the other parent on the weekends with extended periods of time during school vacations."

"I don't think infants should be bounced around," Lisa said, firming her lips. "They need stability and continuity of care."

"They need love and a chance to bond with both parents," Mac said.

Although I could sense his frustration, I was impressed with his control. He had remained calm throughout our discussions, even when Lisa reiterated her demand that he remain single in order to have any role in the babies' lives.

"Perhaps overnight visits could be put off until the babies are six months old?" I suggested.

"A year," Lisa shot back.

I looked at Mac for guidance. He nodded.

"No nights, then. But what about letting Mac have the babies two days a week?"

"I plan to nurse," Lisa said.

"Maybe he could take each baby for one day a week."

Lisa's lip quivered. "He gave up. I don't see why he should expect to spend any time with them."

I started to place a hand on Mac's arm to prevent him from responding, but I need not have worried. His lips firmed, but remained closed.

"Mac, why don't you let me speak with Lisa privately."

After he left the room, I turned to Lisa. "This sort of negotiation can be exhausting, and I know you must be tired. I suggest we call a hiatus until after you give birth."

"Yes. Maybe that would be best." She swiped at her eyes.

"We'll figure out a way to make this work. Do you want me to tell Mac for you?"

She nodded.

Chapter Thirty-Five

Josephine

In preparation for the party at the museum celebrating the unveiling of *Sea Watchers*, Devi, Lill, and I went shopping for new outfits. It was an activity I hadn't engaged in with friends since college when all we could afford was to look. We went to Nordstrom and Devi and Lill insisted I pick my outfit first.

"That's the one, Josephine," Lill said when I came out of the dressing room in a long slim dress in a shade between maroon and magenta.

"I agree," Devi said. "The color is wonderful on you. And you have your choice of how to accessorize."

She whirled away and returned after a moment with a scarf that had touches of turquoise, black, and the same maroon color as the dress. She draped it around my neck.

"Mm-mmm, do you look good, honey," Lill said.

"Okay, I'm set," I said. "Who's next?"

"Definitely Lillian," Devi said.

"My, you have been busy." Lill shook her head at the clerk who was assisting us as the woman lifted three selections from the rack outside the changing room door and handed them to Lill.

Lill disappeared, carrying the three outfits, and Devi wandered off. With the two of them occupied, I took the saleswoman aside and arranged for her to give both Lill and Devi large enough discounts to bring the cost of whatever they picked to under a hundred dollars, putting the remainder on my bill.

"But you have to manage it so they don't suspect."

"Don't you worry about that." She put a finger to her lips and winked.

Lill came out wearing a silky pantsuit with a top patterned in yellow and green. The yellow made her look jaundiced. I shook my head, but Devi was already pushing Lill back into the dressing room.

"Try the tangerine one," she commanded.

"Wow," Devi said this time when Lill stepped out, and I had to agree. The tangerine, a showstopper, perfectly complemented Lill's coffee-colored skin.

Lill pulled on the tag. "It's much too expensive, though."

"Let me see that." The saleswoman stepped forward and slipped her glasses in place. "Hmm. I don't understand this. This should be marked down. You see, it's such a distinctive choice, not many people can wear this color. If you want it, I can let you have it for, say, sixty-five dollars?"

I nodded my approval at the woman who, from the beginning, had seemed delighted at the challenge of dressing up our odd little group.

Lill blinked and then nodded.

"So that takes care of Lill and me." I looked at Devi. "Your turn."

Devi would be easy. She'd look gorgeous in a burlap sack.

The saleswoman, who had already accomplished the most difficult part of her assignment with aplomb—finding flattering outfits for Lill and me—smiled and lifted a dress from the rack outside the changing room.

"I'm thinking this color will not only work with your skin tone, it will blend with what your friends have chosen." She held up a short gown in a pale pinkish-peach color that removed the clash between my dress and Lill's pantsuit.

And when Devi came out of the dressing room wearing it, tears filled my eyes.

"Oh my," Lill said, sounding reverent.

Devi spun, and the skirt dipped and swirled, showing off her lovely legs.

"If that doesn't knock Mac's eyes out, nothing will," I said.

The saleswoman bustled in and twitched the one shoulder, then she checked the tag. "Well, if that isn't odd. This should also be marked down. It's from last season, you see. It was on the wrong rack."

Devi bit back a smile and looked at me. I avoided her glance, concentrating instead on her feet. "You'll need shoes to go with that."

"I will," Devi said with a solemn expression.

She gave me a knowing look and probably would have also wagged her finger if Lill hadn't been standing there. So maybe I wasn't fooling her, but at least she didn't call me on it.

While we changed back into our street clothes, the saleswoman took our credit cards and rang up our purchases away from prying eyes. The game really would have been up if Lill and Devi had seen my bill.

~ ~ ~

The night of the party, Mac, looking spiffy in a lavender shirt and a Vasarely tie in shades of purple, magenta, and blue that I suspected Devi had picked out, drove the three of us to the museum.

He leaned in and whispered in my ear as we walked in. "She's amazing, isn't she?" He nodded toward Devi, who was handing her coat to the coat-check person. "Sometimes I have to pinch myself to make sure I'm not dreaming."

"We're both lucky to have her in our lives," I said.

As we walked into the museum rotunda, Miriam pulled away from a group and came over to us, smiling in welcome. She was wearing a blue gown, and it occurred to me that given this party was in honor of a painting of the sea, perhaps I ought to be wearing blue as well.

"How beautiful you all look," she said. "Good to see you again, Mac. And you must be Lillian." I'd listed Lill as my guest.

"I am indeed," Lill said.

"Come." Miriam took my hand and Lill's. "Everyone is so eager to meet you."

The rotunda was buzzing with conversation. A string quartet played in the background, and waiters circulated with flutes of champagne and plates of appetizers.

Mac snagged flutes of champagne for Lill and me before he and Devi drifted away, leaving us to be introduced to the museum's most loyal members, some of whom I remembered from my days on the board.

"Norman's here," Lill whispered in my ear during one of the few breaks between introductions.

"Where?"

"He's talking to Devi and Mac. Over there." She gestured with her chin to a spot behind us. "And he has a woman with him."

I stiffened but didn't turn around. It hadn't occurred to me he'd be here, although it should have. It was only natural for a man who recovered stolen art for a living to be a member of the art museum. As for having a woman with him, I had no grounds to object, given I'd refused to go out with him.

"If I could ask you all to find a seat, we have a short program to present before we show off *Sea Watchers*," Miriam announced before ushering Lill and me to chairs set in front of a lectern. As Miriam stepped up to the microphone, I realized I'd not asked Devi for details about the program.

Since I was sitting front and center, short of peering around, I couldn't see Norman. But the thought of him being there settled between my shoulder blades like an itch I couldn't quite reach to scratch. It was a relief when Devi and Mac came to take the seats next to Lill and me.

Chewing away at thoughts of Norman, I found most of the program itself was a blur. Miriam introduced me, but she honored my request not to have to speak. Instead, Devi was the one who gave a short history—edited, I was pleased to see—of how she'd first met me and discovered *Sea Watchers* hanging on my wall.

Finally, I was asked to step forward to unveil the painting. While I did that, I took a quick look around but didn't see Norman.

With the painting available for viewing, Miriam turned us loose to continue to mingle, and the quartet once again began to play.

Lill went to the restroom, and as I looked around for Devi and Mac, I saw Norman approaching. My heart rate picked up and my mouth went dry.

"Norman. How nice to see you." And may I just say, thank God there are formulas for dealing with such awkward social situations.

He stepped toward me and took my hand in his. "Jo. You look regal."

Whatever I was supposed to say next eluded me, because standing next to Norman, obviously with him and awaiting an introduction to me, was an attractive woman.

"Jo, this is my daughter, Nan Hollander. Nan, this is Jo."

I extended the hand Norman had just released to his daughter as a gust of relief left me feeling limp.

"So nice to meet you." But didn't she live in Colorado? "You're here visiting?" I struggled to keep my thoughts focused.

"I came for Easter, and I consider it lucky that it coincided with this event. Dad's told me so much about you and how he suspected you of being one of the EKO robbers."

I glanced at Norman, who I was pretty sure was blushing.

"Yes. Not one of my better feats of detection."

"This may be awfully forward of me," Nan continued. "But Dad and I are going to dinner afterward. I'd love it if you'd join us."

"I'm sorry, but I'm here with others."

"They can come too. Admit it; you never get enough to eat at one of these events."

"Norman," Lill said from behind me. She stepped around me and gave him a hug.

"You must be Lillian," Nan said. "I was just inviting Jo to come to dinner with Dad and me. She said she was here with other people, and I expect you're one of them, so will you join us? And are there others? Maybe that young woman who talked about the painting and her escort?" Nan peered around as she spoke. "Oh, there they are."

I turned to see Devi and Mac, hand in hand, coming toward us. They greeted Norman, who introduced them to Nan. When Nan repeated her invitation to dinner, Mac shook his head and turned to me.

"Lisa just called. She's gone into labor, so I need to get back. I'll take you home if you like, but we need to leave now."

"Of course. You get going," Lill said before I could respond. "Josephine and I will be fine with Norman. Are you going with Mac or staying with us, Devi?"

"Why don't you go with Josephine and Lillian," Mac said. "I'll call you as soon as I know what's happening."

Devi nodded but she didn't look happy. Mac took his leave and was jogging by the time he'd reached the coat check.

I turned back to Norman and Nan to find her watching Mac with a frown. "Who's Lisa?"

"His ex-wife."

"Oh." Nan looked from Devi to me.

"Shall we go?" Norman said.

We went.

Nan insisted I sit in front while she, Devi, and Lill sat in the back seat. The three of them—well, mostly Lill and Nan—chatted as we drove to the restaurant. Devi, Norman, and I had little to say either then or during the subsequent meal. Devi was no doubt thinking about Mac and Lisa, and I was distracted by the memory of my reaction to seeing Norman with a woman I'd thought was his date.

In true masculine form, Norman insisted on picking up the check, then he drove Lill and me back to Brookside. I invited Devi to come in with us, but she said she was too tired, so only Lill joined me for a cup of tea and a wrap-up.

"What's going on with you and Norman?" she said with her usual lack of tact.

"Nothing." Which was both literally and figuratively true.

Lill snorted, and I decided it was too bad I didn't care for Scotch. At the moment, I could have used a drink.

"He has a beautiful daughter, doesn't he?" Lill said, changing tack.

"Yeah. A real Chatty Cathy."

"And if she hadn't been, dinner would have been downright gruesome. Devi being upset and distracted, I can buy. But you should be ashamed of yourself, Josephine. You did nothing to make Nan glad she invited us."

"Was that my responsibility?"

"You know, I'm real tired. I'll see you tomorrow. Hopefully by then you'll be over your snit."

And with that, Lill marched out the door, leaving me standing by myself in my quiet, peaceful apartment, feeling dreadful. Because she was right.

I had been rude to Nan and to Norman. And that represented a most unwelcome revisiting of the woman I'd been before Devi, Mac, and Lill entered my life and saved me from myself.

~ ~ ~

When Norman called the next day, I let the phone ring five times before I forced myself to pick it up.

"Jo, I'm calling to apologize for last night. Nan didn't realize—"

"That we aren't friends."

"Something like that. I just wanted you to know I didn't put her up to a stealth attack. I only intended to say hello."

"I know."

"Nan is...well, she's like her mother. Never met a stranger."

I'd tossed and turned for hours last night, and I was feeling old and tired. And, if I was honest, no longer as committed to my peaceful solo state.

"She's lovely. And she has better manners than I do."

That was met with silence.

In desperation, I said the first thing that came to mind. "It's such a pretty day, I was planning to go to Sharon Woods. For a walk." I had to stop to clear my throat. "Maybe you'd like to join me?"

That was met with more silence.

"Nan could come as well," I said.

"I just took her to the airport. A walk sounds good. Do you want me to pick you up or meet you there?"

"I suppose you'd better come here."

"I can be there in twenty minutes."

"Okay. Good."

I clicked off the phone and shook my head, wondering what had come over me. Had I really just invited Norman on...no, it wasn't a date. It was an apology walk. And only because if I didn't make up for being so unpleasant the last two times I saw him, I might backslide further into being the angry woman who first arrived at Brookside. I couldn't stand that woman. And I didn't want to spend another minute being her.

The phone rang again. Devi.

"The babies arrived safely." Devi sounded breathless. "They're two weeks early. A four-and-a-half-pound boy and a five-pound girl. The hospital will be keeping the boy a few days, but the girl can go home tomorrow."

"That's great news."

"Yes. But there's a problem. There were complications and Lisa had to have surgery. She'll be in the hospital several days, they think. So Mac will be taking care of the baby girl until Lisa's released."

"And you'll be helping him?" I guessed.

"I let Miriam know I won't be in next week. But you and I never talked about me taking time off—"

"Don't worry. Take all the time you need."

"Isn't it lucky we got the *Sea Watchers* party out of the way when we did?"

"And it was a terrific party. You did a wonderful job, Devi. I'm sorry I didn't say so earlier."

"We were all distracted there at the end. I'm glad you enjoyed yourself."

We said good-bye, and I went to change clothes for the walk with Norman.

~ ~ ~

172

Sharon Woods is one of my favorite Cincinnati area parks because it has a stream that winds through a shallow gorge surrounded by woods that change with each season.

"The gorge trail or the lake trail?" Norman asked as we entered the park.

"The gorge is my favorite."

He pulled into the parking lot, which was on a steep slant. "Wait, Jo. Let me get the door for you."

He held the door, and I slid out of the car. In the forest, redbuds were just coming into bloom, and violets formed a purple edging along the trail. The stream, which emptied from a small lake, was running fuller than usual due to recent heavy rains, and the forest smelled fresh and clean.

"Do you come here often?" Norman asked.

"Not often enough. My favorite times are spring and fall."

"Mine too. We might have even passed each other sometime." He led the way to the first waterfall overlook and we stood side by side, listening to the music of nest-building birds and water tipping over shelves of rock.

I leaned on the railing, staring at the water. "I want to apologize for my behavior last night."

"That's okay. Neither of us was in particularly good form."

"You see, when I first saw you with Nan, I thought she was your date. And I realized I was sorry I'd pushed you away."

"So in practical terms, you're saying?"

"I've discovered a quiet life isn't all it's cracked up to be. And yes, if the offer's still open, I would like to have dinner with you occasionally, maybe go to a play every once in a while, and," I shrugged, "for walks when the weather's nice."

"Are we talking once a quarter, once a month, every week?"

"I'm not sure, but a month may be too long."

"I see. So, since we had dinner together last night and we are on this walk right now, perhaps another dinner this Friday?"

"I don't understand why you want to spend time with me. Why not someone who's more pleasant and accommodating?"

"Boring. Besides, I knew you weren't pleasant and accommodating from the get-go. Don't forget, Candace warned me before we met."

"And yet you didn't listen."

He shrugged. "At that time, I thought you were the key to the EKO heist. Means I was willing to overlook any peculiarities. But then I realized I enjoy the challenge. My life is so much more interesting with you in it." He paused. "And isn't this where you say I make your life more interesting as well?"

"Do I have to say it?"

He patted my hand and grinned at me. "Not until you're ready."

Chapter Thirty-Six

Devi

The day Mac's infant daughter came home from the hospital, I stayed in the waiting room out of sight while Mac visited Lisa, who was in the same SICU where I'd spent those first days after being shot.

While I was sitting there, one of the nurses who'd cared for me came walking out of the unit and, after a double-take, walked over and grasped my hand.

"Devi. How nice to see you. Just visiting, I hope? You must be because you look terrific. I thought that was Mac in there." Her eyebrows raised in question.

"Yes. His ex-wife just gave birth. He's here checking on her."

"She had the twins, didn't she?"

"She did."

The woman frowned and pursed her lips. "Well, great seeing you, but I better scoot."

With a last squeeze, she turned and walked away, and I wondered what it was about Lisa that had made her frown.

Mac came out then and reported that Lisa was still weak but was recovering, and we walked together to the nursery.

Mac's son and daughter were sleeping side by side, one with a pink cap on its head, and the other, smaller baby, with a blue cap. Once again, I waited while Mac checked in with the nurse and signed the necessary paperwork. Then he came out carrying the pink-capped baby and we walked together to the parking lot. I blinked back tears at the thought Mac and I would never have a baby together.

My resolution not to fall in love with Mac's daughter lasted all of ten seconds after we arrived at the Livingstons' and I lifted her from the car seat. She opened sleepy eyes and peered at me, and I was lost. As I handed her to Mac, I could see he was in love with her as well.

I watched as he lowered his daughter gently onto the bed we'd improvised, since we didn't want to move the crib for the few days we'd have her.

The custody agreement was still pending, but Mac had already agreed on spending only limited time with the babies during the first year, with no overnights. So these few days, while Lisa recovered and Mac's son put on enough weight to be discharged from the hospital, were an unexpected gift.

Or maybe a curse, I thought as I rocked Mac's daughter to sleep after I'd fed her. Lisa was too weak to attempt nursing the babies, so we'd bought the formula recommended by the pediatrician who'd cared for the babies in the hospital.

Mac would be returning to work in the morning, leaving the baby with me during the day. And it would no doubt set Lisa's recovery back substantially if she knew I was helping to take care of her daughter.

"When will you choose a name?" I asked him.

"We agreed that we each get to pick one baby's name. I figured I'd pick the boy's name, and she'd pick the girl's, but..."

"It's hard to keep calling her 'she' or 'baby girl,'" I finished for him.

"Yes."

"Any thoughts?"

"Not really. What about you?"

"It's not my place. And you do realize Lisa wouldn't want me within twenty feet of either her son or her daughter."

"That may be, but without your help, I'm not sure how we'd be managing right now."

"It's going to be so hard to give her back."

Mac came and stooped down beside us, and his hand reached out to cup his daughter's tiny head. "Yeah." He sighed. "You know, I do have an idea for a name—Lily. It was my grandmother's. What do you think?"

"I love it, but you'd better make sure it's okay with Lisa. Here, why don't you lay her down." Reluctantly I handed the baby to him, already knowing it was going to be painful when I handed her over for the return to Lisa.

Chapter Thirty-Seven

Mac

I left Lily behind with Devi the day I went to pick up Lisa and Toby from the hospital. The first words out of Lisa's mouth were, "Where's Lily?"

"I left her with a babysitter."

"I hope it's someone reliable."

"Very. No need to worry. Shall we go get Toby?"

She nodded and took a seat in the mandated wheelchair. Unlike Devi, Lisa didn't ask me to push her around so she could say good-bye and thank-you to everyone who'd taken care of her. But then Lisa had been here only five days, not two weeks like Devi. Although, even if Lisa had stayed longer, I doubt she'd have bothered. It was yet another unwelcome insight I wish I'd had before I asked her to marry me.

The nurse smiled at Lisa as she handed Toby over. "We're going to miss this little guy. Good luck to you."

Shortly after the twins' births, I was notified the house I'd been renting had sold. Although I had until the end of the month to vacate, I'd seen it as an opportunity and moved Lisa's and the babies' belongings into Devi's old apartment. Which was where I took Lisa and Toby now.

"You can't be serious, Darren. You're moving me into your old girlfriend's apartment? There's something seriously wrong with this picture."

"I told you, when I discovered the house had to be vacated, I decided to let you have the apartment."

"Then where are you living?"

"I've found another place. In Montgomery."

"Why can't we live there with you?"

"We're divorced, Lisa. We need to live separately."

"So, who pays the rent for this dump?"

"It may be small, but it's not a dump. And you're responsible for the rent. Or I am indirectly, I suppose. And you can always look for another place."

I was holding Toby, and he chose that moment to wake up and start fussing. Lisa grabbed him out of my arms. Harrumphing, she walked over to the couch, sat down, and opened her blouse.

"I didn't realize you were nursing."

"I can't feed them both. But one of the nurses helped me get started with Toby." Her expression softened as Toby nursed.

"I, ah," I said, my throat constricting. "I'll go get Lily, shall I?"

"Yes. Do that. And then you can help me unpack." She glanced at where I'd piled the several boxes she hadn't unpacked since arriving on my doorstep. "How long before you're back?"

"Thirty minutes?"

"Fine," she said, her attention refocused on Toby.

At the Livingstons', I found Lily's equipment and clothing stacked by the door and Devi sitting in the rocking chair I'd appropriated from one of the bedrooms. She was holding Lily, and when she looked up at me, her eyes were swimming with tears.

"It's time, isn't it?"

"Yes. But you can stay there with her until I get everything in the car."

She nodded.

I took my time loading the car, making more trips than were necessary—knowing that Devi had fallen in love with Lily, and parting with her was going to hurt. Finally, I could put it off no longer.

"I have to take her, Devi."

She nodded. "I know." She handed Lily to me.

I couldn't bring myself to look at Devi, knowing I'd want to cry too.

At Lisa's place, I first carried Lily inside. She was sleeping, so I unwrapped her and laid her next to Toby who was also asleep. Lisa came to hang over the crib.

"You ought to take a nap while you can. I'll get the rest of Lily's stuff. And then I need to get back to work."

"Sure. Fine."

I watched as she walked into the bedroom, before unloading the rest of Lily's supplies. Then with a last look at my sleeping son and daughter, I walked out, pulling the door closed.

~ ~ ~

When my shift ended, I drove to the apartment to see how Lisa was doing. I could hear a baby crying, so I knocked, then used my key to open the door. Lisa was nursing Toby while Lily lay red-faced and screaming in the crib.

"Thank God you're here," Lisa said.

I picked Lily up and she stopped crying, briefly. I got a bottle of formula out of the fridge, warmed it in the microwave, then mixed it thoroughly before checking the temperature on my wrist.

As soon as the nipple touched her lips, Lily stopped crying, and with little hiccups of distress, started sucking.

"Aren't you the expert," Lisa said, her tone sarcastic as she lifted Toby to burp him.

"Lily's trained me well." I took a seat on one of the kitchen chairs, thinking I needed to buy Lisa a more comfortable chair to nurse.

"It's only been a few hours and already, I'm overwhelmed. I don't know how I'll manage two babies by myself. Even one baby..." She sighed. "I don't think you made it to your car this morning before Toby woke up. He's eating every hour."

"And Lily eats every two to three hours," I said.

"Yeah." She yawned.

"Tell you what. Why don't you take a nap. I'll keep an eye on them for you. Here. Let me get Lily set and then you can hand me Toby."

I moved to the couch and grabbed a pillow to prop Lily up. Then Lisa handed me Toby. I laid him on my knees and used one hand to make sure Lily was secure. It was awkward, but doable.

As soon as Lisa handed over Toby, she went to lie down. When Lily finished her feeding, I burped her, then, with a baby in each arm, I placed them on the improvised changing table, changed both diapers, and laid them in the crib. Then I stepped outside to call Devi to let her know I wouldn't be home until late.

While Lisa and the babies slept, I thought about Lisa coping with two babies on her own. Given the amount of effort it had taken Devi and me to care for Lily the past five days, I couldn't imagine how Lisa would manage. Especially as she was also recovering from their birth and the complications that followed.

I cooked spaghetti and ate, leaving Lisa a portion. When Toby began to fuss an hour later, I warmed a bottle for him to give Lisa more time to rest. He wasn't happy with the bottle, but his cries were much less vigorous than Lily's, and eventually I got him to take the formula without waking Lisa.

She didn't come out until both Lily and Toby awoke together an hour later.

"I gave Toby formula an hour ago. You could nurse Lily now, and Toby next time."

"Toby needs it more than Lily," she snapped. She picked him up and walked over to the couch with him. I picked up Lily. Anticipating, I had formula already warmed to room temperature. Within a minute, both babies were feeding.

"We're a good team," Lisa said, looking over at me.

"I can't be here all the time."

"I know. You have to work. But if you slept here..."

"Lisa, I can't do that."

"Can't or won't? The bed's big enough for the two of us. What? You think I'm going to seduce you? For Pete's sake, Darren."

I shook my head. "I'm not sleeping here."

"True. You spend the night here, you won't get much sleep." She rubbed her eyes. "You can't just leave me alone. I need your help."

"How about this?" I swallowed, worrying it was too soon and maybe I should wait until she spent at least one night alone with the twins. "Since you aren't nursing Lily, I could take her for the night. Bring her back in the morning, on my way to work."

Lisa sat blinking at me. "I think it makes more sense for you to spend the night here, Darren."

"No. Sorry. I'm not doing that." If I did it once, I'd be stuck until both babies slept through the night. And who knew when that might be.

Maybe Toby sensed her tension, because he stopped nursing and fussed, and Lily did as well. Or perhaps it was sympathetic fussing. One of them setting the other off.

"Fine," Lisa said. "Take her home, but only for the night."

"We'll be back at seven."

~ ~ ~

When I walked in carrying Lily, Devi put her hands up to her mouth, then stretched out her arms. I placed Lily in them.

"What's happening, Mac?"

"Lisa didn't think she could handle both on her own. So it was bring Lily here or spend the night there. And you know what an easy choice that was."

Devi closed her eyes, then opened them and smiled at me. "I've been so scared."

"Of what, love?"

"I knew she'd need help. I...well, I'm just so glad you're here. And Lily. I missed Lily."

"It was only a few hours."

"I know. I'm crazy about your daughter, Mac."

"Yeah, me too."

"How's Toby?"

"Doing well. Eating every hour, which is why Lisa's exhausted. And why she agreed to this arrangement."

"Did you tell her about us?"

"Not yet. But I will soon."

~ ~ ~

I returned Lily before work, and when I arrived at Lisa's the next evening, I found both babies and Lisa crying. Toby and Lily were in their crib, and Lisa was in the bedroom, her face pressed into a pillow, howling.

Softly, I closed the door on her and went over to the babies. Toby seemed the most distressed so I picked him up first, then I bent over Lily and ran a finger over her head. She stopped crying, her tiny fist moving toward her mouth.

I placed Toby in his infant seat, moved that next to Lily, and got her propped up next to him. Then I went to the kitchen to warm bottles of formula. With them in their seats, I managed to feed both at once, although Toby once again objected to the bottle.

While I was doing that, the bedroom door opened and Lisa stepped out, her face splotched red from crying, her hair lank.

"I can't do it, Darren."

"Why don't you take a shower? It will make you feel better."

"The only thing that's going to make me feel better is a good night's sleep. You have to stay, Darren. I can't do it alone. I can't."

I lowered both bottles and went over and put my arms around her. "Come on. Let's get you in the shower. Then you can sleep while I take care of them."

"Both of them?"

"Take that shower, and then we'll talk about what to do next."

Behind us, both babies started to fuss. After giving Lisa a nudge in the direction of the bathroom, I returned to the living room to finish feeding the twins. After they finished, I burped them, then I carried Toby to the kitchen and ran water in the sink to give him a bath. Devi and I had bathed Lily, but I suspected Lisa had been too harried to bathe Toby.

After changing both babies into fresh outfits and placing them back in their cribs, I collected the dirty clothes and took them downstairs to the laundry room. Back in the apartment, I found the cupboards mostly bare, so I called to have a pizza delivered and added grocery shopping to my growing list. When I checked on Lisa, I found her in bed fast asleep.

By the time the pizza arrived, Toby was ready to eat again. Because he was so tiny, I managed to use one hand to hold both him and the bottle while I ate with the other. When Lily awakened, I went and shook Lisa awake.

"You need to eat, and we need to talk."

"Don't wanna eat or talk. Just wanna sleep." Her words were slurred, her eyes at half-mast. Under other circumstances, I would have suspected she was drunk.

"How about I take both Toby and Lily with me for the night?"

"Do what you want. Just leave me alone." She rolled away from me. I waited a moment to see if she'd say anything else, but it appeared she'd fallen back to sleep.

Lily was working up to a major meltdown. I got out a bottle of formula and sat down to feed her. With my free hand, I called Devi. "Can you come?"

"Of course. But won't Lisa—"

"Lisa's asleep, and I could use your help."

"I'll be right there."

By the time Devi arrived, Toby was awake again and fussing. Devi took one look at me with Lily and went over and lifted Toby into her arms. I pointed to the formula sitting on the counter, and she picked that up and came to sit next to me to feed Toby.

"What's happening?"

"Lisa's exhausted. If it's okay with you, we're on full twin duty for the night. My thought is that as soon as they finish feeding, we'll take them home."

Devi pursed her lips. "Okay."

"Can you work half days for a while?"

"Because?"

"I think we'll be on twin duty at least half the time for the foreseeable future. And you're going to need extra rest."

"What about you?"

"I'll be okay." Although the truth was after six nights of broken sleep, I was already tired. Both Devi and I were. And adding Toby to the mix, with his more frequent awakenings, even taking turns, it was going to be grueling.

"Did you tell Lisa about us?"

I shook my head. "She was too exhausted to hear it."

We bundled up Toby and Lily and took them home. As soon as the babies were settled, Devi and I went to bed, even though it was only seven thirty.

"Best plan is to sleep when they do," Devi said.

I lost track of our ups and downs during the night. By morning, it felt like we were taking care of more than two babies, and both Devi and I were in the same shape Lisa had been in the night before. One at a time, we called into work.

I had both personal and vacation time accumulated, although I would normally provide notice before taking it, but when I explained the situation to the chief, he told me he didn't want to see me for the next two weeks.

We changed and fed both babies, and all four of us went back to bed.

What awakened me next was my cell phone. I grabbed it without checking the ID to keep it from disturbing Devi.

"Darren? Where are Toby and Lily?"

"Just a sec." I crawled out of bed, walked into the bathroom, and closed the door. "They're with me," I said, trying to keep my voice down.

"Why are you whispering?"

"They're asleep."

"I need to nurse Toby."

"He just ate. Tell you what. I'll let them sleep an hour and then I'll bring them back."

"Don't you have to go to work?"

"I'm taking time off."

"You are?"

"Listen, you relax, eat breakfast, and I'll be there in an hour."

"O...kay."

When I opened the bathroom door, Devi was lying in bed, wide awake.

"That was Lisa. I arranged to take the babies back in an hour. I want you to come with me."

She gulped and then sat up, swinging her head to move her hair out of her eyes. "Guess I better get ready then."

I left her showering while I went to the kitchen and scrambled eggs and made coffee. When she came in dressed, I took my turn in the shower. By that time, both babies were awake.

"We need to move fast. Lisa wanted to nurse Toby this go-round."

Devi nodded, and together, we got the twins into their car seats. Ten minutes later, we pulled up at the apartment, where we each took a crying baby.

Lisa must have been listening for us because she opened the door as we reached it. With a quick startled glance at Devi, she grabbed Toby out of my arms and disappeared into the bedroom.

When she emerged thirty minutes later, she ignored Devi while she changed Toby and put him down in the crib. Then she turned to the two of us. We were sitting next to each other on the couch with Lily lying on my knees.

"So, Darren. It appears news of your breakup was greatly exaggerated."

"We never did break up. But I did let you think we had."

"Why?"

"I figured you'd never grant me custody if you'd known Devi and I were together."

"Devi, hmm. I don't believe we exchanged names the last time we met."

"No, we didn't."

"So, *Devi*. Could you excuse us? I think Darren and I need to talk."

"We do. But Devi's a part of this. She's been helping me take care of Lily, and last night she got up as many times as I did to take care of Toby. You need to know that whenever Toby and Lily are with me, they'll be with Devi as well."

Lisa shook her head and started to speak, then stopped and cleared her throat. "Well, I guess I owe you a thank-you, Devi."

"I'm happy to help."

"I don't think we'll make it through the next few months without Devi's help."

"So, what are you proposing?"

"I'm off work for the next two weeks, so Devi and I could take care of Toby one day and Lily the next. Then once they're sleeping for longer periods, we can figure out a different schedule."

"What about nights?"

"I'm thinking twenty-four hours at a time."

"Don't you think it would be better if you take Lily full-time and I keep Toby since I'm nursing him?"

"Alternating gives us all a chance to bond with both Toby and Lily. And that way you can nurse Lily part of the time."

She stood and paced, then whirled to face us. "Oh, all right."

She was crying. Devi lifted Lily from my knees and nodded toward Lisa. I stood and gave her an awkward hug.

"I feel so awful, Darren. Here I thought I'd be thrilled. Instead, I feel like I'm going crazy."

"You're still recovering your strength. And you're not getting enough sleep. It will get better. And you have us to help you."

"Yeah, right. My husband and his girlfriend."

Over Lisa's shoulder, I looked at Devi. She shook her head, warning me not to respond to Lisa's comment.

"So." I held Lisa at arm's length. "If we start the arrangement today, do you want us to have Lily first or Toby?"

Her shoulders slumped. "I suppose you better take Toby." Her lip quivered.

I pulled her back into the hug. "It's going to be okay. Why don't you rest? Lily won't need to be fed for a couple of hours."

"Just go!" She pulled out of my arms and stomped out of the room.

Devi, who'd been holding Lily, carried her over to the crib. I picked up Toby and, with sighs of relief, we left Lily and her mother alone together for the first time.

Chapter Thirty-Eight

Josephine

Devi and Mac stopped by on a Saturday as they were in the habit of doing. Sometimes they had Toby with them, but today they had Lily. I'm not much of a baby person, but Lily and Toby had both managed to wrap me around their tiny fingers within seconds of my meeting them.

"How's Lisa?" I asked.

"Doing better than she was," Devi said. "Mac and I are both in good shape, and we find taking care of a baby together tiring. So I know how exhausting it must be for her."

"Is this a permanent thing? You with one twin, Lisa with the other?"

Mac shook his head. "Doubt it. I expect that once they're sleeping through the night, Lisa will want them both with her."

I glanced at Devi. The look on her face made it clear she'd be sad when that happened.

"Although I also suspect she'll be happy to let me pitch in on my days off," Mac added.

"And have you two set a date yet?" Devi had been wearing the diamond circlet on her right hand, but it had recently shifted to her left hand.

She looked at the ring, then at me. "Lisa doesn't know we're engaged."

"And you're afraid of what she'd do if she knew?"

"She tried to make the custody arrangement contingent on Mac's remaining single."

"You didn't agree to that, I hope?"

"No," Mac said. "We're still discussing terms. But I think she's accepted the fact Devi isn't going away."

"Any advice, Josephine?" Devi said.

"Not even a glimmer, I'm afraid."

In my view, this latest situation is yet more proof the universe is inherently unfair. Mac and Devi are such good people. They deserve to experience the full joy of their love for each other and a baby of their own. Instead, Mac was being pulled away by Lisa and the twins, and Devi couldn't have a child.

As I was pondering their dilemma, there was a sharp rap on the door. Mac went to answer while I continued to cuddle Lily.

"How predictable to find you here," the visitor told Mac.

"Jeff. What are you doing here?"

"What indeed. May I come in?"

I nodded to Mac, who moved aside. Devi took Lily from me, and I stood to face Jeff.

He was gripping a bouquet of roses, obviously purchased from Kroger, as if it were a club. Under his arm was a manila envelope.

"Mother. These are for you. Happy birthday. And could you ask your guard dog here to give us some privacy?"

I ignored the bouquet thrust in my direction until he gave up and laid it on the dining room table.

"Anything you have to say can be said in Mac and Devi's presence." And thank God Mac and Devi were here.

"Well, I want them to leave."

"And I want them to stay. And since this is my home, I get to decide."

Jeff stood blinking for a time, then he cleared his throat. "I have papers for you to sign."

"What papers?"

Jeff glanced at Mac and his Adam's apple bobbed. "A durable power of attorney and a health-care proxy. Best to get them taken care of. After all, you're not getting any younger."

"No, I'm not. But I've already made arrangements."

"Without consulting me?"

"Why would I consult you?"

"Because I'm your son? Your only relative."

"That's true. And if I had any intention of involving you, I would have consulted you. But as it is—"

"Wait. You've named a durable power of attorney, and it isn't me?"

"That's correct."

"Then who is it?"

"Why, it's someone who cares about me and has my best interests at heart. Someone I can trust will never try to railroad me into a competency hearing so he can get his hands on my assets."

"Are you going to tell me who?"

"No, I don't believe I will. And if you recall, I've already informed you that I accept full responsibility for myself. That means there's no need for you to insert yourself in my affairs ever again."

"That's cold, Mother."

"Not as cold as you attempting to have me declared incompetent when I'm perfectly capable of taking care of myself."

"I apologized for that. A misunderstanding, based on incomplete information. I was worried about your state of mind. This is different."

"Of course it might seem that way to you. What I see is you making another attempt to control me."

Jeff started to speak, then stopped and cleared his throat. I walked over to the table, picked up the flowers, and thrust them back into his hands. "Unless and until you're willing to make a good-faith effort to treat me with respect, I'd prefer not to see you."

After I closed the door behind him. I stood for a moment, trying to catch my emotional balance before turning back to Devi and Mac.

Devi stood and handed Lily to Mac, then she came and put her arms around me.

"I'm so sorry you had to witness that," I told her.

She held me a moment longer before walking me over to the sofa where she sat next to me and took my hand in hers. "What happened between you?"

"Thomas, my husband. He had no respect for me, and he taught Jeff...from the time he could talk...and nothing I did could change it. It just got worse as Jeff grew up." I looked at Mac. "Don't you ever do that. No matter what problems you and Lisa may have, don't ever say anything to Toby or Lily." I found I was shaking my head, struggling not to break down.

"You have my word," Mac said, jiggling Lily, who had started to fuss.

"And mine," Devi said. "I'm so sorry, Josephine."

"Yes. Well, thank you both. I don't know what I'd do if I didn't have you as friends."

Devi patted my hand, and I gulped and managed a couple of shaky breaths. "You know, I believe it was still my turn to hold Lily."

Mac smiled and came to place the baby in my arms, Devi went to make tea, and we all tried to push aside the dark aura Jeff had cast over us.

~ ~ ~

The day after Jeff's visit, I responded to a knock on my door to find Norman standing there, holding a bouquet that was definitely not from Kroger.

He questioned me with his expression, and I motioned for him to come in.

"Rumor has it that someone had a birthday? Although I consider it odd that someone failed to mention it."

"Lill told you?"

"She called and said you might need cheering up. Something about an unpleasant encounter?"

"With my son."

"That's what I assumed, although Lillian was the soul of discretion."

"Aside from immediately calling you, you mean. Sounds like I need to find someone else to confide in."

I'd still been upset after Devi and Mac left, and I'd told Lill the whole story, but my son was a subject I was still trying to avoid with Norman.

I raised my eyes to Norman's to find he was watching me closely. "It's a beautiful day," he said. "Maybe you'd rather walk than talk. And I know just the place for it."

~ ~ ~

Norman parked in the same garage by the ballpark we'd used when we went to lunch together the first time. It was a short walk from there to the river promenade where we soon reached a line of aluminum swings—updated versions of the old-fashioned porch swing. Norman snagged one of the two vacant ones for us.

It was soothing to swing slowly back and forth and just people watch. There were runners, cyclists, whole families, couples, old and young, all enjoying the spring sunshine. Since it was Sunday, there wasn't much traffic on the river— some jet skis, a couple of power boats, and a single tug plowing a deep furrow through chocolate-colored water, shoving a covey of barges downstream.

For a time, we swung in silence, and Norman's quiet presence and the shadows rippling over my face wiped away the last of my upset from Jeff's visit.

Most of the time, I avoided thinking about Jeff and grieving the permanent fissures in our relationship. But seeing him yesterday had reopened old wounds that gradually began to scab over as we moved back and forth.

"Are we friends, Jo?" Norman asked after a comfortable silence.

"Yes. I believe so."

"Good." He reached over and took my hand in his. "Then you trust me?"

"I don't understand."

"To be careful with your confidences. And your heart?"

I had to think about that. While I did, we swung in silence.

"Yes. I guess so."

193

"Okay then. I'd like you to tell me about your son, and why seeing him upsets you so much."

I tried to pull my hand away. After initially resisting, Norman let me go.

"It's a long story." I wondered how much of a relief it might be to tell someone everything.

"I have plenty of time," Norman said.

When I began speaking, my words were halting at first as I told him how I'd failed to notice until after the wedding how controlling Thomas was.

"I planned to go to graduate school to study economics, and then I hoped to find a university position. But Thomas refused to let me either go to school or to work. So I became a desperate housewife. One who pinched pennies to play the stock market. But I made too much money, and that meant Thomas found out. He forced me to turn everything over to him except for a small amount I was able to keep hidden from him."

I shook my head, trying to shake away the hollow feeling that accompanied any memory of that interaction. Although it took place a half century ago, it was still as fresh in my mind as if it happened yesterday.

"From that point on, Thomas treated me like a servant."

"Oh, Jo." Norman reached for my hand and I let him have it. "Why didn't you leave?"

"I thought about it. But I knew Thomas would fight me for custody of Jeff. I stayed because of that. When Thomas began encouraging him to be disrespectful, I hung on, hoping things would get better. By the time I realized they never would, I didn't have the energy to leave." I stopped speaking, knowing I'd just told Norman a lie. But the truth was something I'd barely acknowledged, even in the silence of my own thoughts.

However, I was talking to a man who made a living finding lost things. That meant he wasn't the best candidate to buy a half-baked story.

"The truth is…" I pictured myself standing on a building ledge high above a street. One step, a few more words, and Norman would be out of my life. But if I didn't speak, I'd be accepting his friendship, knowing his good opinion of me was based on lies.

"The truth is..."

"You didn't want Thomas to force you to sell the painting during a divorce?"

"Yes. Well, partly. At that time, I had no idea the painting would one day be worth millions. But yes. He'd already taken so much from me, I couldn't bear the thought of him taking anything more. But I'm not proud of that decision. I should have left. You see, there was someone else I loved. A man..." *Daniel.*

The only person I'd ever told this story to was Devi, when we were in the hospital together after Devi was shot.

"You had an affair." Norman's words sounded certain but calm.

"Yes. I bought *Sea Watchers* from a gallery in New York. The owner of the gallery and I met whenever we could manage it for the next twenty years."

"And your husband never knew?"

I shook my head. "I visited Daniel when Thomas went on one of his golf outings or on a business trip. He never called when he was away. In reality, he paid little attention to me even when he was home."

"What about now? Why aren't you and Daniel together?"

My throat closed and my eyes filled with tears.

Norman squeezed my hand. "Sorry, Jo. Sometimes I put my foot in it. He died?"

I nodded.

"I am so sorry."

"Now you know why I'm not a good risk as a friend."

"And the reason for that is?"

"Isn't it obvious?"

"Does anyone else know this story?"

"Devi does."

"And did Devi cast you off as a friend when you told her?"

I shook my head because I didn't think I could manage to speak.

"Good to know. I have a high opinion of that young woman. Glad to hear it's deserved."

We continued to swing. Finally, Norman sighed and squeezed my hand, which he'd held throughout my confession.

"Here's what I think, Jo. You lived in an intolerable situation for a long time. And to cope you had to find ways to survive. Your way was keeping who you were a secret. And you had an affair. That tells me you're no saint. And may I say 'thank God' for that? Because I'm no saint either, and I think it would be exhausting to live with one."

"L-live with one?"

"Figure of speech. At least, until you're ready."

"I can't promise I ever will be."

"I know. But I plan on sticking around anyway."

He talked then about Nan and her visit, and that he was planning to go to Colorado to see her and her family more frequently than he had in the past.

"We have only one open case at the moment, and my partner and I have agreed that once we wrap it up, we're going to sell the agency to our associate."

"So you were serious about retiring."

"Being at Brookside helped me think it through. Give it a test run, in a way. I've also decided I'll be selling my house as soon as I can get it ready. That's one of the reasons Nan came to visit. To help me clear out her mother's things. Now, I just have to clear out the rest."

"Have you decided where you're going to live once you sell your house?"

He shook his head. "I didn't want to make too many decisions at once. Tell me, how did you decide on Brookside?"

"I didn't. My son decided."

"Without consulting you?"

"It's one of his most endearing characteristics." I swallowed. That had sounded like the old, angry me. "Sorry. Sometimes I can't help getting snarky about him."

"I can understand why you would be, if he didn't ask your opinion."

"When I first moved in, I couldn't wait to get out of there."

"What changed your mind?"

"A lot of things. The most important was that Lill, Devi, Mac and I became friends. Although the thought of moving also became less appealing as time went on."

We continued to swing in comfortable silence. Then Norman patted my hand.

"You know, Jo, I don't need any promises from you, but do you have any objection to plans?"

"Plans?"

"I'm thinking about taking a trip."

"You are? Where to?"

"I'm still deciding. Do you like to travel?"

"I've done so little, I'm not sure. I suppose it depends on the specifics."

"Here's one specific. Would you be interested in coming with me?"

I froze, and without realizing it, my foot dragged and the swing stopped its regular back and forth.

"It's okay," Norman said. "I don't need an answer today. But I'd like you to think about it. It does seem like a reasonable next step. Lunches, dinners, plays, walks in the park, confidences."

I wondered how I'd ever thought it was a good idea to push this man out of my life. Still, I hadn't given up entirely on being cautious, despite the fact I'd been trying to limit my caution strokes whenever I wrote a list or a note. Not making a big effort or production of it. Still...

"I'd like to know where this trip is going before I think about it."

"Is that a maybe?"

"Maybe."

"Hmm. A *maybe* maybe. Progress. Okay, how about this? What appeals to you the most—Europe, South America, Asia, Australia, Africa, or Antarctica?"

"You're talking a major trip then."

"What? You were thinking Niagara Falls?"

"Niagara Falls is very nice. People travel from all over the world to visit there."

"They do. But I'm thinking something more..."

"Challenging?"

"You could say that. Can we narrow it to a continent at least?"

"Okay. Australia."

"Anything specific you'd like to see?"

"Let's see. How about Sydney, the Great Barrier Reef, and Uluru."

"You realize that's like going from Florida to Massachusetts and then to Denver?"

"Well, you asked. And they must have airlines, don't they?"

"They do. Are you saying if I plan it, you'll go with me?"

"Remember, you've been warned I can be difficult."

"It's one of the things I like most about you, Jo. You're also straightforward."

"Not always. But about the trip. Okay. Why not?"

He stopped the swing with his foot and turned to look me in the eye. "You're not playing me here, Jo. You'll really go to Australia with me?"

"You plan; I'll pack."

"It's a deal. Although, we will need to wait for the warmer weather in November or December to visit. Maybe we can pick somewhere else to go this summer?"

"I thought you planned to go to Colorado, to see your daughter."

"You're right. How about you come with me? We can use it as a test run. See if we're compatible travel buddies."

I smiled to myself. "Okay."

Clearly, my confession and Jeff's visit had put me in a reckless mood. And if Norman still wanted to have a relationship with me after knowing all my secrets, then it was time I got to know his family, and that made Colorado a good starting point.

"My only condition is that we have to check dates with Mac and Devi. I am not missing their wedding."

"You've got it. And, Jo?"

"Yes, Norman."

"The best is quite possibly still to come, you know."

Chapter Thirty-Nine

Devi

What with helping Lisa with Toby and Lily, Mac and I didn't manage to set a wedding date until the end of the summer. We picked the Thanksgiving break so my parents could attend.

Our plan was to keep the whole thing small and simple as Mac still had nightmare memories of his elaborate wedding with Lisa. I was happy for the excuse to forgo most of the fancy wedding stuff—choosing a color scheme, writing our own vows, picking a play list, taste-testing cakes and entrees, arranging for doves to be released. All of that and more would have been required if I'd married William Garrison, a thought that still made me shudder.

But when Josephine discovered our minimalist approach, she conspired with my mom, and the two of them begged permission to help with the macro planning of venue, menu, flowers, and cake.

Since not only was I busy helping care for the twins, I was also organizing an exhibit of Edward Hopper paintings for the art museum, I was happy to turn over wedding planning to their capable hands. My suspicion was that Josephine not only did most of it, she also paid for most of it.

But this was one time I didn't want to argue with her. I wanted to be Mac's wife, and I willingly went along with whatever it took to make that happen.

Josephine arranged for the ceremony to take place by candlelight in the rotunda of the art museum on Thanksgiving Eve. A string quartet and a harpist alternated throughout the ceremony and dinner that followed. The photographer had orders not to be intrusive, and mostly, he wasn't.

It was all beautifully baroque and entirely perfect.

Josephine's wedding gift, besides the planning, was to pay for a nanny to help Lisa with the twins for the ten days Mac and I would be away. Although Lily and Toby did mostly sleep through the night, Lisa was still accepting our help. Thus the need for the nanny. Neither Mac nor I wanted to take a chance Lisa might discover she didn't need us.

My parents paid for a honeymoon to anywhere we wanted to go. We picked Sedona, because what we wanted most was to be together in a place where we could take long walks, eat leisurely dinners, and stay in bed until noon.

Norman escorted Josephine to the wedding. I'd had my suspicions about them ever since they spent a month together in Colorado this summer, and as I stood next to Lillian, watching the two dancing a slow, intimate waltz, I considered my suspicions confirmed.

"Um-hmm. Sure is nice to see Josephine got her confidence back," Lillian said.

"I've always thought Josephine was one of the most confident people I've ever met."

"She may have fooled you, sweetie, but she didn't fool her Graphoanalyst." Lillian's tone was smug. "Oh my, did that girl have caution strokes. Longest ones I ever saw."

"But she doesn't anymore?"

"Does that look like caution to you? Hmmph. Too old for romance, indeed."

Mac came up and whispered in my ear. "Would you like to dance, Mrs. McElroy?"

I turned, smiling, and he took me in his arms.

"I want to cut in on Jo," Mac said.

Since Norman's been in the picture, Mac's taken to calling Josephine "Jo" as well, but it doesn't feel quite right for me to do it.

"I haven't had a chance to talk to her today," he added.

"Looks like we'd be interrupting something."

"Does look that way. Not going to let that stop me, though. I have privileges, after all. I am the groom." Mac maneuvered us over to Josephine and Norman, and he tapped Norman on the shoulder. "Mind if I cut in?"

"Not if I get to dance with the bride," Norman said.

"Only a temporary trade, mind you."

The two men grinned at each other, then Norman swept me away.

"You know, I was hoping to talk to you today," he said. "You see, I owe you a thank-you, and it's long overdue."

"For?"

"For being Jo's friend, and continuing to be her friend after she told you about Daniel."

"Wow. She told you about Daniel?"

"She did. But then she said she didn't expect I'd want to still be her friend. The only thing that convinced her she was wrong about that was my reminding her you'd still wanted to be her friend after she told you about Daniel. So you see, both Jo and I owe you. Big-time."

"That is so good to hear."

"That we both owe you?"

"Given all Josephine has done for me, you better believe it."

"She loves you, you know."

"And I love her. So you better take excellent care of her."

"That's my intention."

The music drifted to a close, and I looked over to see Mac dipping Josephine over his arm. She came up laughing.

And then my husband and my dear friend walked over to Norman and me, and Josephine took my hands in hers.

"Devi, thank you for marrying Mac, and thank you for letting me help you plan."

"I think I'm the one who should be thanking you. Everything is perfect. And totally stress-free. You're like the fairy godmother of wedding planners. Thank you so much." I hugged her and whispered in her ear, "I love you so much, Jo." For once the "Jo" felt right and natural.

"Darling girl, I love you too, and I don't think you can imagine how grateful I am to have you in my life."

After a moment, we stepped apart, both of us wiping tears from our eyes.

It was destined to be one of my favorite wedding pictures.

<<<>>>

About the Author

The books Ann loved most as a child were those about horses. After reading Mary O'Hara's Wyoming ranch stories, she decided she would one day marry a rancher and own a racehorse, although not necessarily in that order.

Since it was clear to Ann, after reading *My Friend Flicka* and *Green Grass of Wyoming*, that money could be a sore point between ranchers and their wives, not to mention racehorses don't come cheap, she decided appropriate planning was needed. Thus she appended a "rich" to the rancher requirement.

But when she started dating, there were no ranchers in the offing, rich or otherwise. Instead, Ann fell in love with a fellow graduate student at the University of Kansas. Not only does her husband not share her love of horses, he doesn't even particularly like them, given that one stepped on him with deliberate intent when he was ten.

After years in academia, Ann took a turn down another road and began writing fiction. Her first novel, *Dreams for Stones*, was published by Samhain Publishing on Christmas Day 2007, and has now been re-released in electronic and print formats. The protagonist is both a university professor and part-time rancher—proof perhaps that dreams never truly go away, but continue to exert their influence in unexpected ways.

Those unexpected influences continue to play a role in Ann's succeeding books, including this one.

A Note to Readers

I hope you enjoyed *The Babbling Brook Naked Poker Club – Book Two* and will want to keep in touch with me by signing up for my mailing list.

If you sign up you'll receive an occasional newsletter that will include insider information about my writing process, the stories behind the stories, new release notifications, and recommendations of books I think you may also enjoy.

You will also receive a link to a short story as a thank-you.

All you have to do is go to my website (AnnWarner.net) to sign up. And be assured, I hate spam so I will never share your email address with anyone else.

Also...if you enjoyed this novel, I'm hoping you'll be willing to take a few minutes more to share your opinion with others on the novel's Amazon page. Having a minimum number of reviews is a requirement for me to be able to publicize the book on book discovery sites like Fussy Librarian, Kindle Book Reviews etc. Although longer reviews are preferred, even a brief statement of your opinion helps prospective readers find the book.

Thank you so much!

Acknowledgments

Although writing a novel requires solitude, no book gets published in isolation. Of the many people who have contributed to the process for this novel, I'm especially thankful to the following:

Delores Warner, who provided invaluable expertise to ensure the Graphoanalysis details in this novel are correct. Any errors in interpretation are mine. Thank you so much, Delores.

Pam Berehulke, who ensures that my grammar, punctuation, and timelines are perfect, although since I have a tendency to tinker, errors may have tiptoed their way in after Pam gave the book her imprimatur. If you should find an error in this novel, be assured I introduced it. Mea culpa, Pam.

All my early readers/reviewers who have helped in the final polishing of this novel: Juli Townsend, Margaret Johnson, Criss Roberts, Melissa Trumpower, and the members of the Women's Fiction Critique Group on FaceBook: Gail Cleare, DJ Dalasio, Kate Murdoch, Jennie Ensor, Muriel Canfield, Pat MacAuliff, and Karin Davies.

And to all those who have written to comment on my stories, especially those of you who have told me my novels have been a source of comfort or distraction during tough times, thank you!

My gratitude as well to everyone who has posted a review. Your kindness makes it easier for me to make others aware of my novels.

And above all, thanks to my husband who lights up my life and makes it possible for me to be a full-time writer.

Also by Ann Warner

All Ann's novels are available in print and electronic editions

Memory Lessons

Glenna Girard has passed through the agony and utter darkness of an unimaginable loss. It is only in planning her escape, from her marriage and her current circumstances, that she manages to start moving again, toward a place where she can live in anonymity and atone for the unforgivable mistake she has made.

As she takes tentative steps into the new life she is so carefully shaping, she has no desire to connect with other people. But fate has other ideas, bringing her a family who can benefit from her help if only she will give it. And a man, Jack Ralston, who is everything she needs to live fully again, if Glenna will just let herself see it.

Absence of Grace

Available as a free download. Information at
AnnWarner.Net

The memory of an act committed when she was nineteen weaves a dark thread through Clen McClendon's life. It is a darkness Clen ignores until the discovery of her husband's infidelity propels her on a quest for her own redemption and forgiveness. At first, her journeying provides few answers and peace remains elusive. Then Clen makes a decision that is both desperate and random to go to Wrangell, Alaska. There she will meet Gerrum Kirsey and learn that choices are never truly random, and they always have consequences.

Counterpointe

Art, science, love, and ambition collide as a dancer on the verge of achieving her dreams is badly injured. Afterward, Clare Eliason rushes into a marriage with Rob Chapin, a scientist. The marriage falters, propelling Clare and Rob on journeys of self-discovery. Rob joins a scientific expedition to Peru, where he discovers how easy it is to die. Clare's journey, which takes her only a few blocks from the Boston apartment she shared with Rob, is no less profound. During their time apart, each will have a chance to save a life. One will succeed, one will not. Finally, they will face the most difficult quest of all, navigating the space that lies between them.

Love and Other Acts of Courage

A freighter collides with a yacht and abandons the survivors. A couple is left behind by a dive boat.

These are the dramatic events that force changes in maritime attorney Max Gildea's carefully organized life, where, win, lose, or settle out of court, he gets paid and paid handsomely. As he represents the only survivor of the yacht sinking and gets involved in the search for the couple missing from a dive trip, his reawakening emotions catapult him into the chaos of sorrow and joy that are the necessary ingredients of a life lived fully.

Doubtful

Doubtful Sound, New Zealand: For Dr. Van Peters, Doubtful is a retreat after a false accusation all but ends her scientific career. For David Christianson, Doubtful is a place of respite after a personal tragedy is followed by an unwelcome notoriety.
Neither is looking for love or even friendship. Each wants only to make it through another day. But when violence comes to Doubtful, Van and David's only chance of survival will be each other.

Dreams for Stones — Book One
Dreams Saga

Indie Next Generation Book Award Finalist
Available as a free download. Information at
AnnWarner.net

A man holding fast to grief and a woman who lets go of love too easily. It will take all the magic of old diaries and a children's story to heal these two.

Caught in grief and guilt over his wife's death, English professor Alan Francini is determined never to feel that much pain again. He avoids new relationships and keeps even his best friend at arms' length. His major solace is his family's ranch south of Denver. Children's book editor Kathy Jamison has learned through a lifetime of separations and a broken engagement that letting go is easier than hanging on. Then she meets Alan, and for once, begins to believe a lasting relationship is possible. But Alan panics and pushes her away into the arms of his best friend. Now the emotions of three people are at stake as they struggle to find a way to transform their broken dreams into a foundation for a more hopeful future.

Persistence of Dreams — Book Two
Dreams Saga

Lost memories and surprising twists of mystery. Alan, Kathy, and Charles's story continues. The ending of his love affair with Kathy and an arsonist seeking revenge are the catalysts that alter the shape and direction of Charles's life. Forced to find both a new place to live and a way to ease his heartache, Charles finds much more as he reaches out to help his neighbor Luz Montalvo. Helping Luz, forces Charles to come to grips with his fractured friendships and the fragmented memories of his childhood.

The Babbling Brook Naked Poker Club Book One

Available as a free download. Information at
AnnWarner.net

A painting worth millions, valuables gone missing, a game that is more than a game. And that's only the beginning as an elderly widow befriends a young woman and tries to prevent her from making the same mistakes she has made.

The Babbling Brook Naked Poker Club Book Three

Josephine Bartlett is back, joined by a colorful cast of friends: her partner in mystery-solving, Lill Fitzel, flamboyant ex-beauty queen, Myrtle Grabinowitz, former attorney/current novelist, Philippa Scott Williamson, Brookside's thief, Edna Prisant, good friends Devi and Mac McElroy, and last, but not least, love-interest Norman Neumann.

When new resident, Lottie Watson, loses at Naked Poker, she tells a bizarre story about her husband disappearing in the LA airport. Josephine and Lill, intrigued enough to investigate, discover there are more ominous goings-on than a simple disappearance. Meanwhile, Josephine ignores the mysteries of her own heart.

All the Babbling Brook books are available in print, large print and electronic editions from Amazon.

Made in the USA
Coppell, TX
21 September 2020

38500429R00127